Travel Note Sketch Book

建築旅行

旅行速寫簿

鄭政利 Cheng, Cheng-Li

天空數位圖書出版

自序

人的一生少不了旅行，在文明歷史之初，人類的生活狀態就是旅行。狩獵採集者為了生存，在大地上永不停歇地追逐流浪，游牧民族追逐牧草和水源，在馬背上奔馳漫遊、移動遷徙，旅行是生活也是生存的現實。現代社會仍然有人為工作為生活到處旅行，然而更多的人是為了豐富心靈、追逐夢想、經歷冒險，尋求生命中的新體驗而旅行。現代人的旅行憑藉進步的交通工具與發達的資訊技術，確實可以讓人無遠弗屆且旅行深度豐富。平淡的生活總會激起旅行的慾望，旅行有時候的確令人著迷，旅行途中所有遇到的人事物景，總是能夠為渴求的內心帶來啟發與感動。旅行中的體驗是來自心靈的，是可以真切感受到自我成長與蛻變的過程。旅途中走過大山與大水，見識過雄偉與壯闊，體驗過博大與精深，會讓我們更謙卑、更知足，更接近靈魂深層的自己。在旅行中常有獨處的時光，有時候既浪漫又愉悅，有時候卻既艱辛又徬徨，但往往在這過程中可以碰觸到最真實的自己。在一段又一段的美好旅行中，我看到的比記得的多，但記得的卻比我所看到的更深更遠。旅行是一生的修行，旅行中所有的體驗與記憶都化成了生命的養分，滋潤了自己也豐富了人生。旅行也是一種冒險，不只是用雙腳和眼睛，還得帶上靈魂和夢想。人生如果沒有美好的冒險與夢想，那就什麼都不是了。人的一生也可以說是一段生命的旅行，走過大半歲月人生，旅行中一路上我看人看建築看風景也看自己。這本旅行速寫簿收錄了人生旅途上，每一段對人對建築對風景感動的當下，也有莫名的抽象情緒，透過畫筆不經意擷取的瞬間，希望給自己留下一個值得回顧的記憶，也分享給喜歡的人。

目錄 Content

人物 People

旅行中觀察形形色色的人，各式各樣的人種、穿著、打扮、表情，是最有趣的體驗之一，優雅的、粗獷的、匆忙的、安詳的、焦慮的、喜悅的……每一張臉都有一個當下的故事，每一個眼神都流露出當下的情感……

Observing all kinds of people during travel, all kinds of races, clothes, dresses, expressions, is one of the most interesting experiences, elegant, rough, hurried, serene, anxious, joyful.... Every face has a story of the moment, and every look in the eyes reveals the emotion of the moment...

2013.04.26
ROMA.
Coffee Greco. 250 years
2013.03.27
Water Wise conference
Oxford Univ. LMH.
2013.03.18
Water Wise Conference
Oxford. LMH. UK.

2013.04.26. ROMA
Priest. in Spanish stairs
MILANO. ITALIA
Oxford. UK.
LMH. Talbot Hall

Oxford. Uk.
Great. British. museum. UK
Working woman.

Galleria dell Accademia
FIRENZE. MUSEE
St. MARCO Plaza, Venezia
Coffee. music. party to midnight.
ROMA.

British Museum. UK
Africa Room. Galleries
2012.09.05
MAYA. British Museum
2012.09.05

2015.08.09
2015.08.09
2015.08.09
2015.08.09
2015.08.09
絲路
2015.08.09
2015.08.09

Antoni Gaudi
Nepal. Kathmandu
Nepal

Nepal Woman
Kathmandu. Airport.
Pohkara.
Nepal.
In Chopin's footsteps around
Warsaw. Poland.
Dresden.
Station

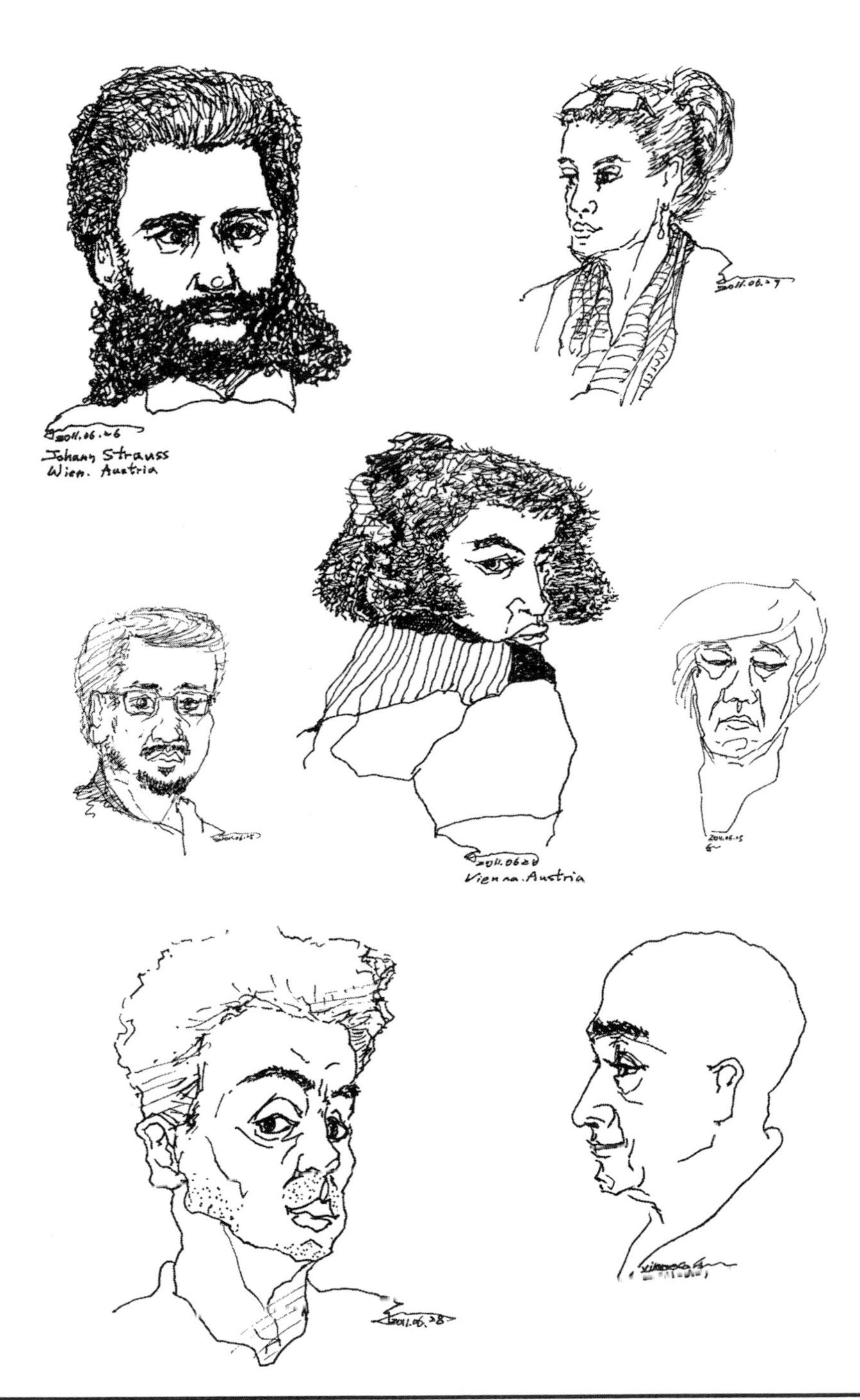
2011.06.26
Johann Strauss
Wien. Austria
2011.06.28
Vienna. Austria

2014.04.19
Chivay. PERU
2014.04.27. Yagua Family Leader
2014.04.16
Peru. Lima
2014.04.17
Lima. Peru
Larco Museo.

2017.07.16
2014.04.26. Amazon
MAURICIO
Tour Guide in Arequipa
Peru 2014.04.18
2014.04.19
Chivay, Peru.
ROMA.
Amazon Dancing Boy
FOTO DI PAOLO BUSATO ©

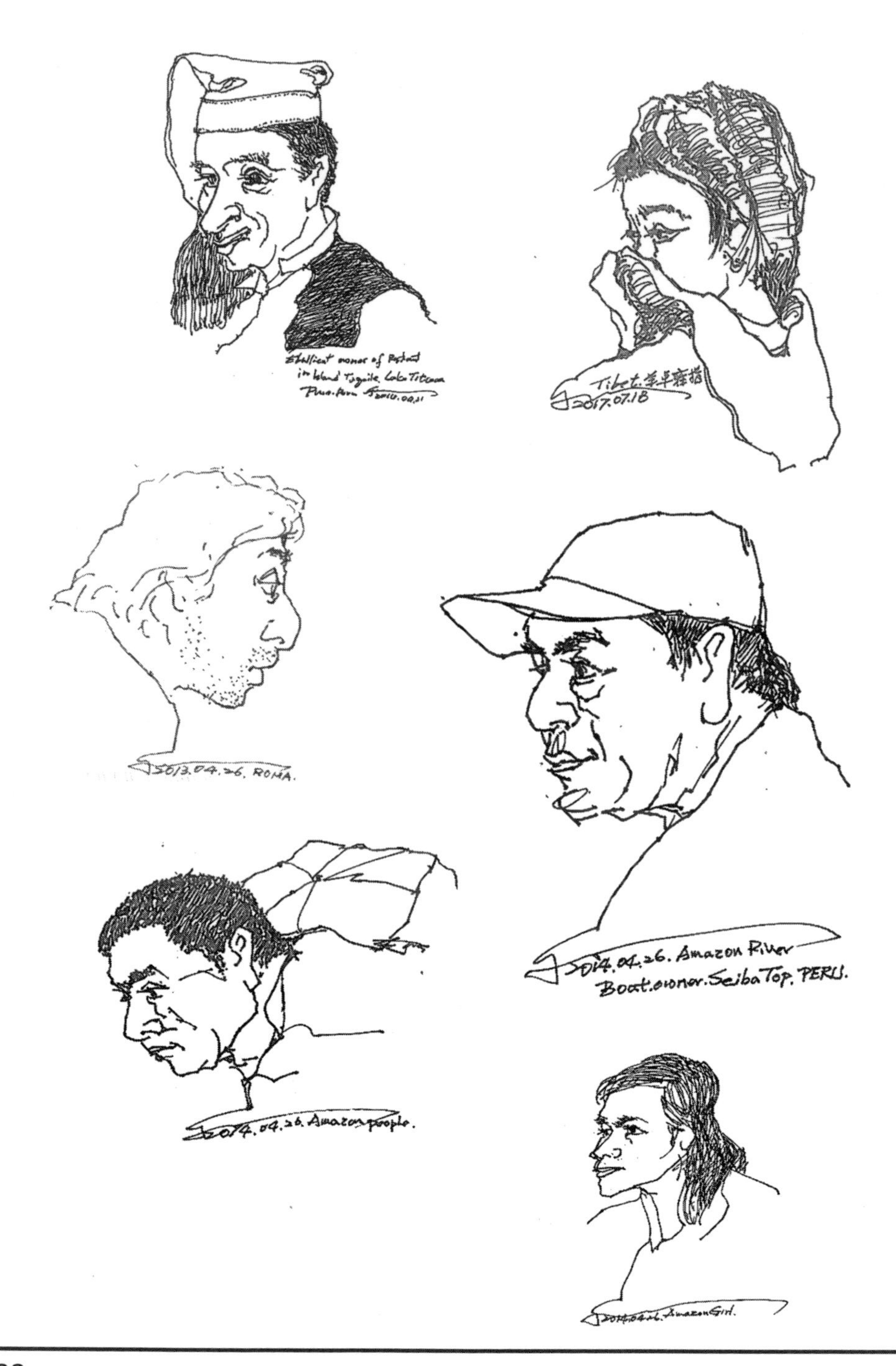
2017.07.18
2013.04.26. ROMA.
2014.04.26. Amazon River
Boat.owner. Seiba Top. PERU.
2014.04.26. Amazon people.
2014.04.26. Amazon Girl.

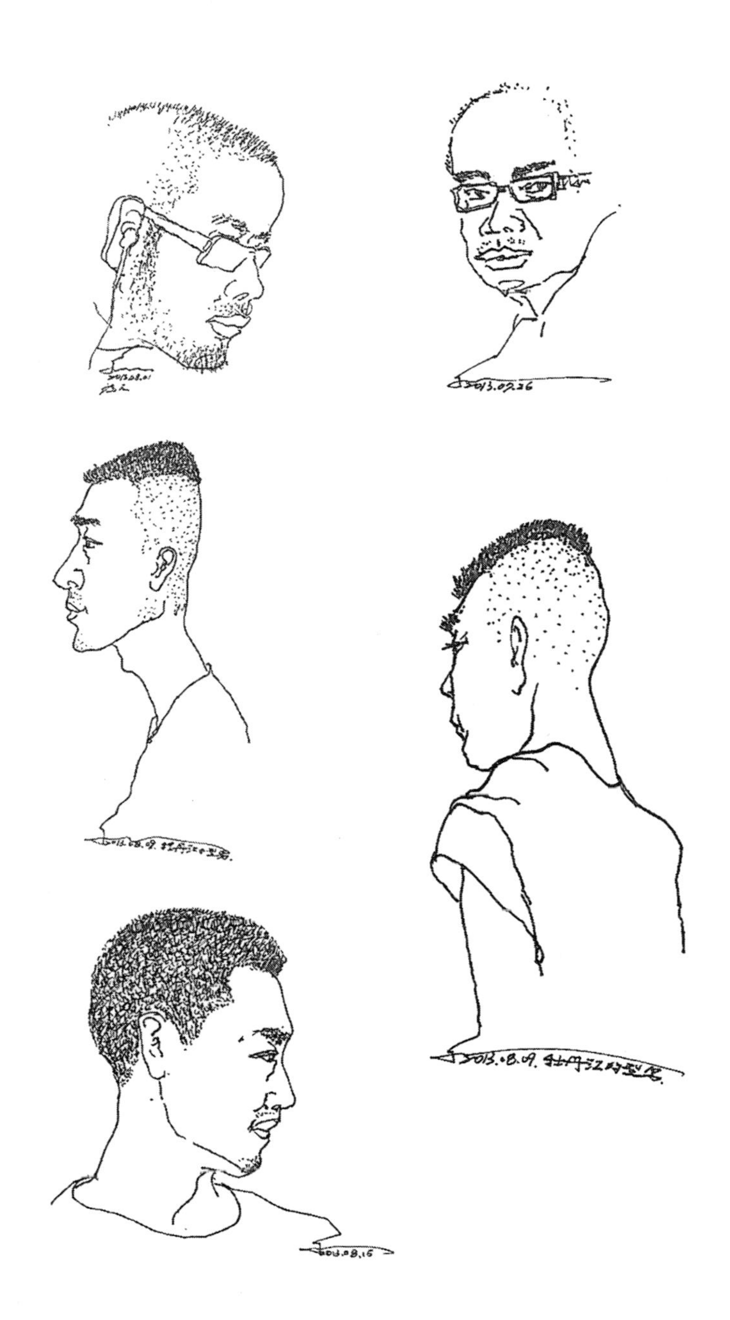

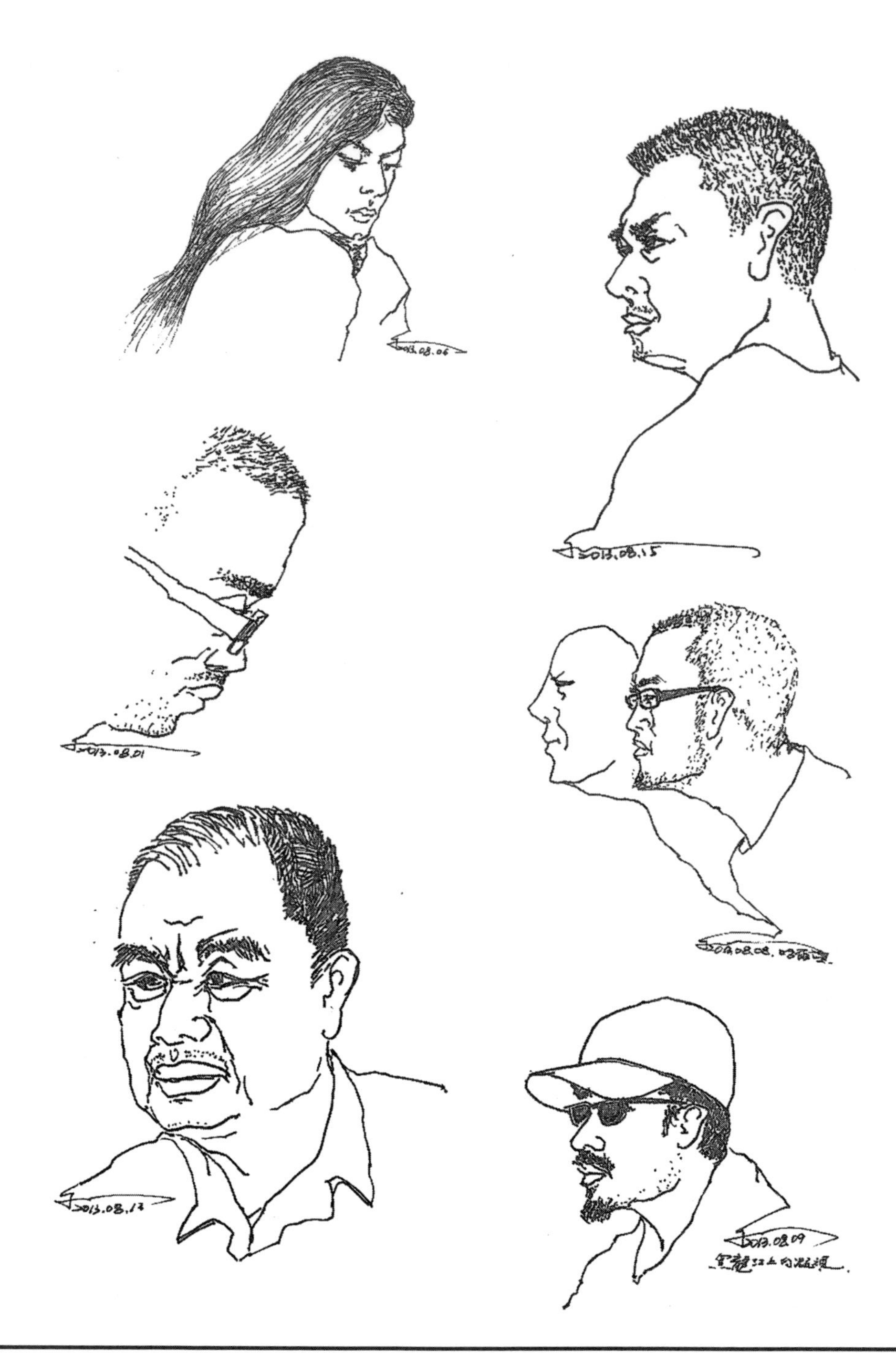
2013.08.06
2013.08.15
2013.08.01
2013.08.08.
2013.08.13
2013.08.09

Laurence
2014.02.22
A brave girl from France, she
came to travel this world. from India.
and will continue to Asia countries
and South America.
We met in HoiAn. VietNam.
2014.02.22
Vietnam. Hanoi
Oldman.
A old woman walk hard
on the way. Hoa Lu-Tam
Vietnam.
2014.02.22 My Son, HoiAn.
Viet Nam.

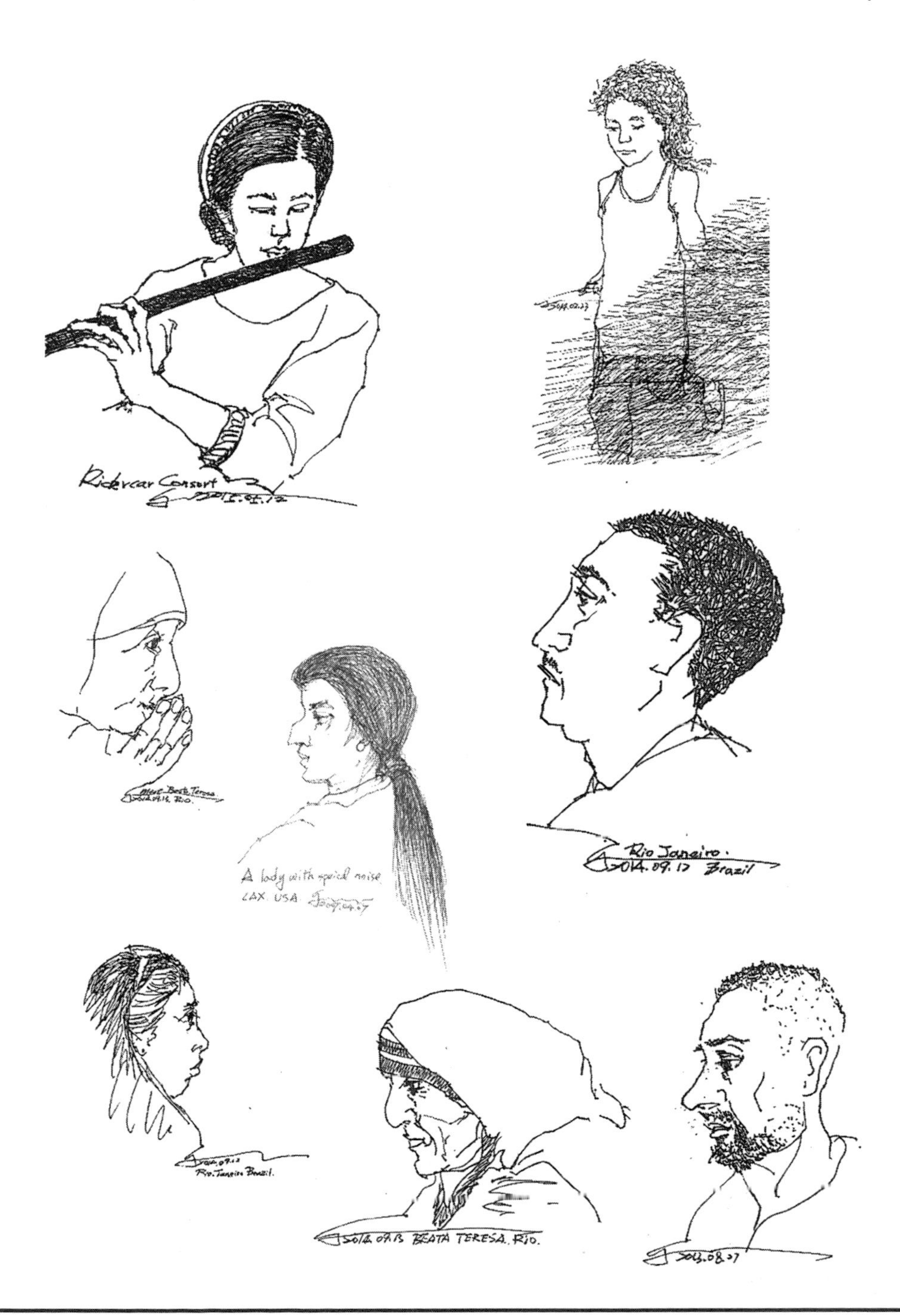
Rickercar Consort
A lady with special noise
LAX USA
Rio Janeiro
2014.09.17 Brazil
2014.09.13 BEATA TERESA. Rio.

Rio. Brazil
2014.09.12
Fresno. CA. USA
Tibet.
2017.07.18
Tibet
2017.07.19
2017.07.16
San Francisco. USA.

2009.09.12
Street construction worker
2007.04.04
09.09.14
2009.09.14
2006.07.08

A lady in
Reef Fleet
Terminal. Cairns
2010.11.13
man on boat. 2011.11.17
2009.09.16
上海 田子坊
2010.07.11

2015.08.20. 北京798藝術區
2015.08.10. 維吾爾族女。
烏魯木齊.新疆.絲路之旅
烏魯木齊.走在街上的
維吾爾母女。2015.08.10
2015.08.20.北京.798
Firenze. Italy
2016.09.04. Budapest.
Fatál Restaurant.

2015.08.15.
2016.08.26.
2016.08.26. Vienna Airport
waiting to Kosica.
2016.08.26.
2016.08.26. Vienna.
Airport waiting for Kosica

2017.08.16
2018.09.04 Fatál
BUDAPEST.
2017.08.13.
Helsinki. Finland.
2017.08.18.

Art. Museum, 2008.06.02, LACMA.LA.
2008.04.20
Phoenix
2008.05.14
LAX.Airport..
2008.05.14
LAX.Airport.
2008.05.14
LAX.Airport.

Lunch
William Keith. 1838-1911
Old master of California
"He who is a blessing for
his time is a blessing for
all time." U.C. Berkeley.
second visit. 2008.05.02
2015.09.22
Magisch Panorama
秋田由來の美人
北国旅の2. 酒田
2001.02.11
戴帽子的女人. 背影
2001.02.21
Rotterdam

2005.09.22
Den Haag.
MAASTRICTS
Fontainebleau, France.
楓丹白露
2005.07.20
MAXTRICK.

电车上人们的速写
东京
2001.02.17
低头读书的电车乘客
2001.02.16
东京电车上人们的速写
2001.02.17

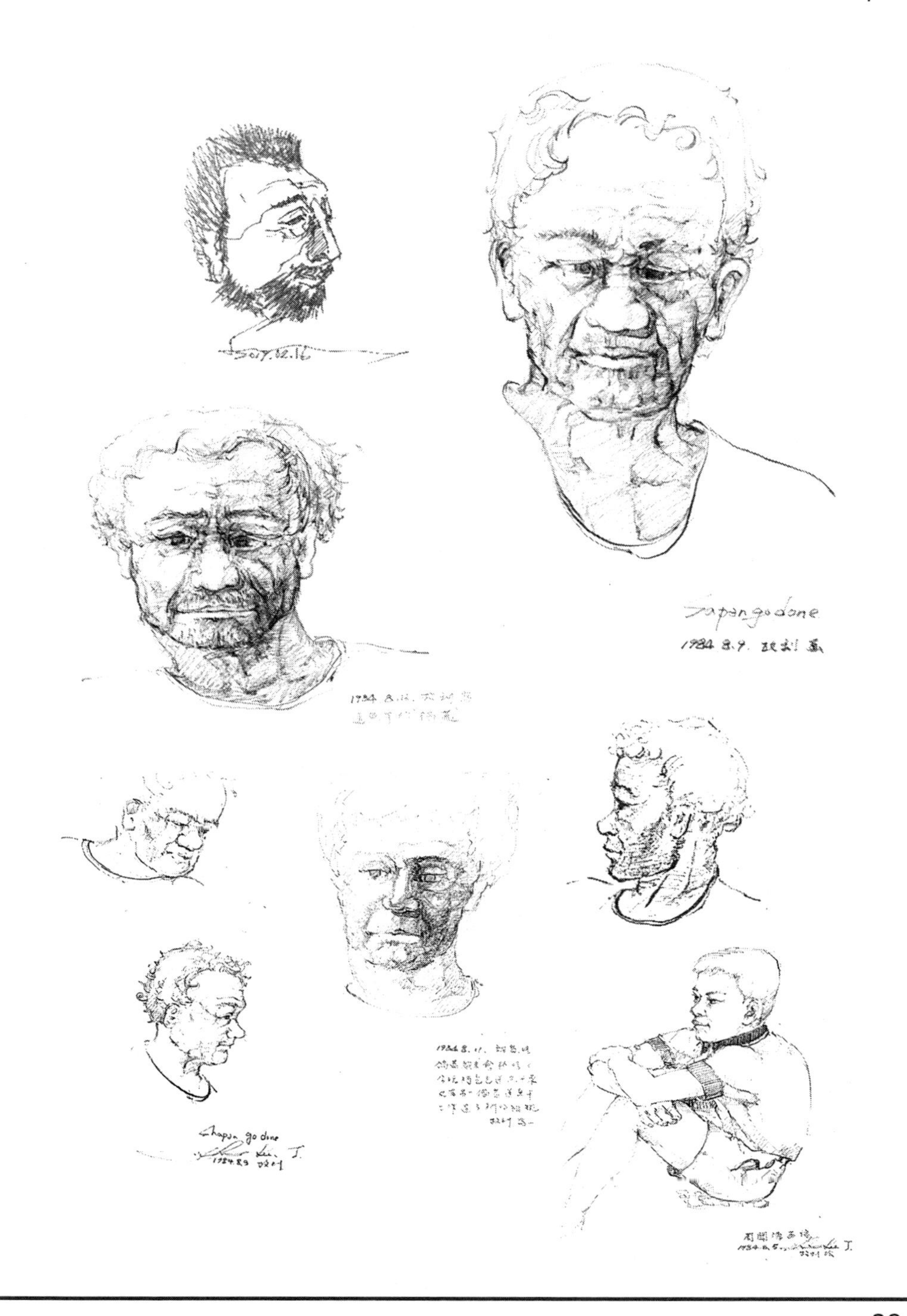

87.4.13
三毛
87.2.27

John. E. Engelberger in working, NJ. Tower.
Tommy. Pforzheim
98'.09.26
Profile of Professor. Galowin
Woman on the Train
to Karlsruhe
John. E. Engelberger working in Tower. NJ.

People sleep at airport
Les Misérables
Imperial theatre
A man with beautiful girl friend in boat

Hat Lady 2003.01.02
Madrid. Spain
98'. 8.5
98.8.10
Some Lady. I see in Sevilla.
Spain 2003.01.6

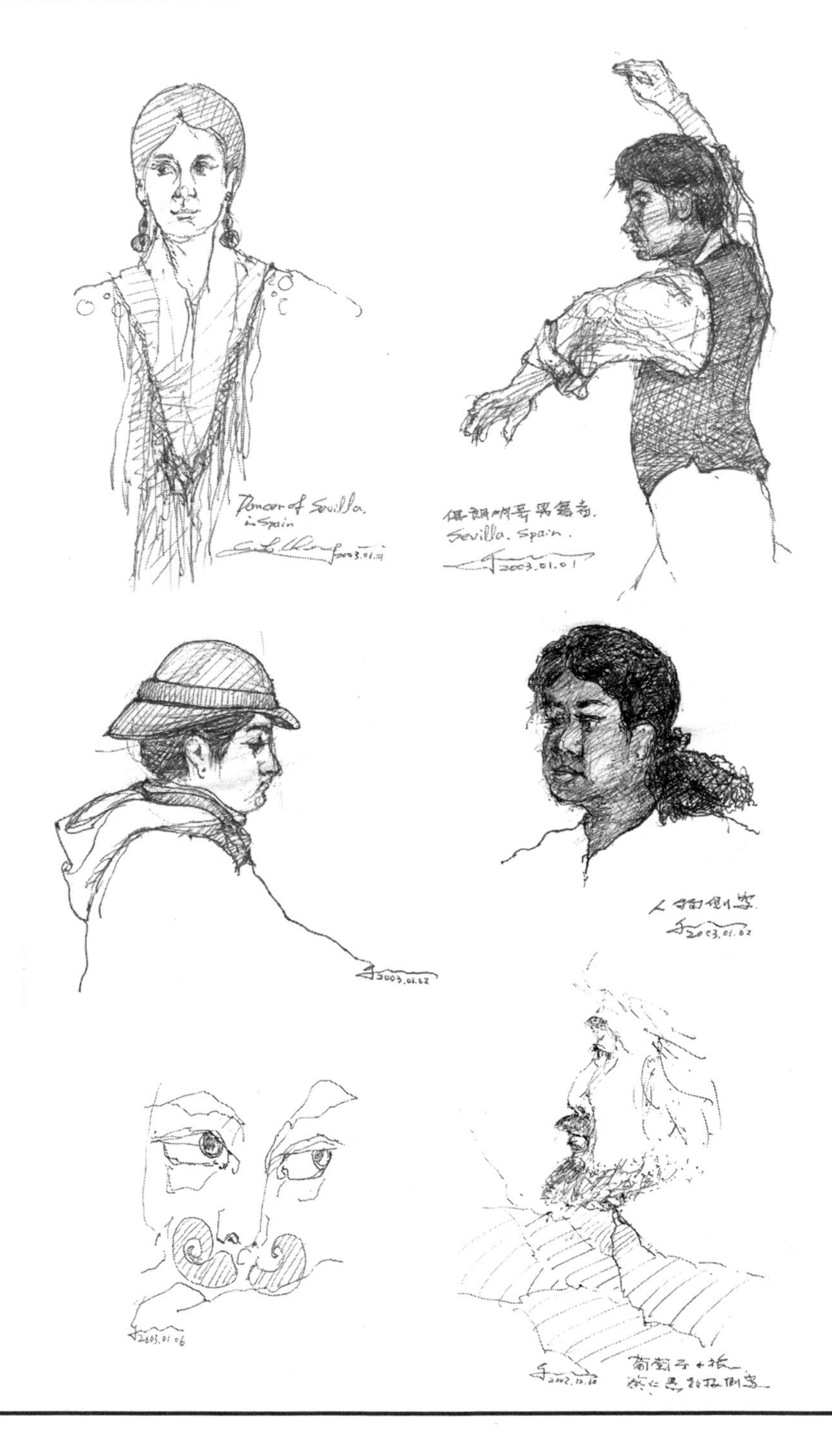
Dancer of Sevilla.
in Spain
2003.01.01
佛朗明哥男舞者.
Sevilla. Spain.
2003.01.01
2003.01.02
人物側寫.
2003.01.02
2003.01.06
2002.12.30

2003.01.07
4 CATS. Coffee time. Barcelona
One man with long face.
佛朗明哥女舞者

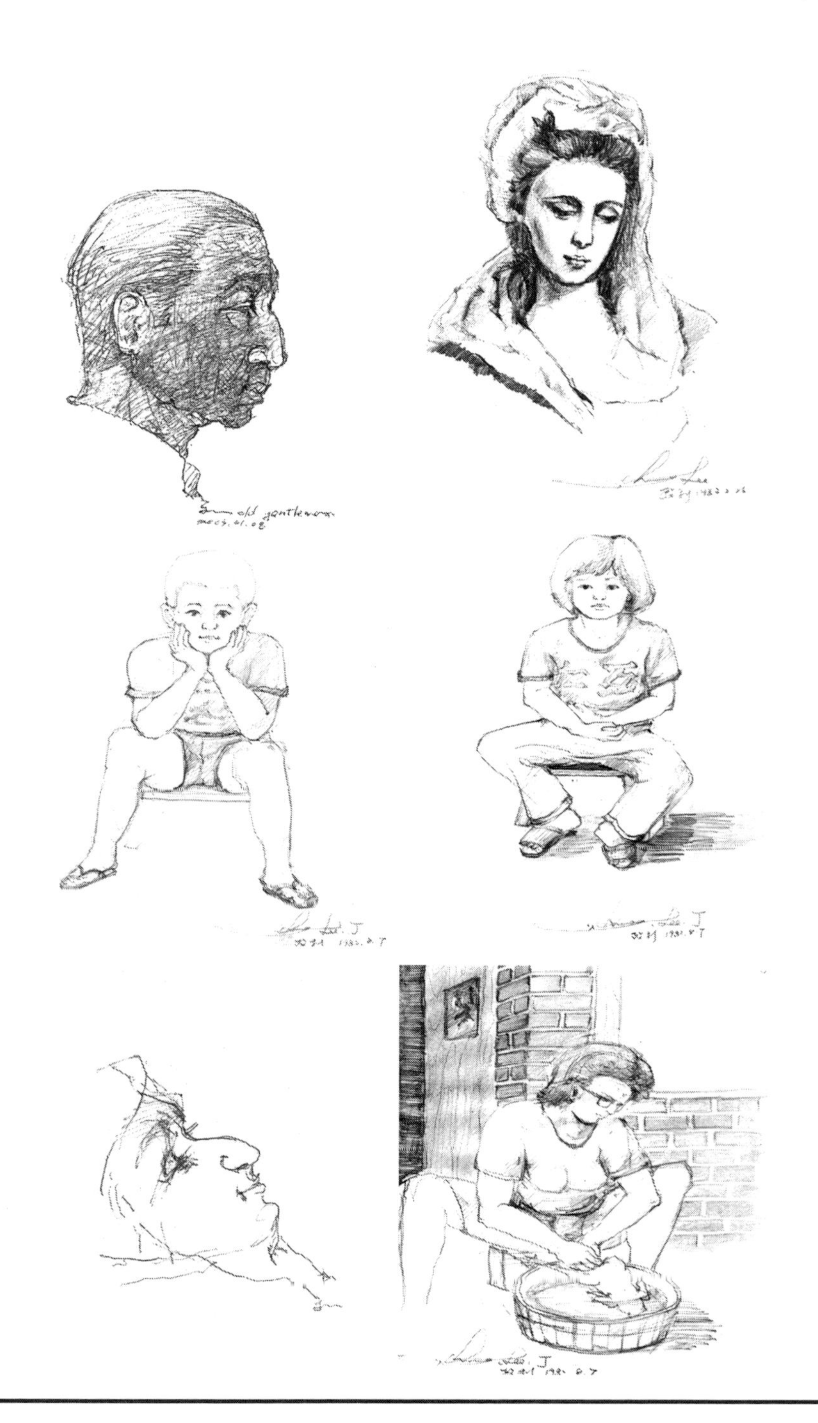
old gentleman

Buffalo can weigh 2000 pounds
and Sprint at 30 miles per hour,
may appear tame but is wild,
unpredictable and dangerous.
The wild Buffalo
I met on the road
in Yellowstone Park
Surprising and exciting
A wonderful contact.
Yellowstone
駱駝臉

2014.04.26
Amazon Animal.
2014.04.26. Amazon.

Fasion Dancer. 2006.04.06
Mckintosh 2006.04.09

三十年的經過，門前的小樹苗已
成綠蔭，鄉間的小路鋪上柏油，
當年新蓋的房子，只剩斷垣殘牆。
三十年的歲月，不長，也不短。
夢想的翅膀，引領著小鎮裡
放牛的小孩，從鄉間走進都市，
從故鄉走過他鄉，也留下旅途
數不盡的悲喜痕跡。
如今，放牛的小孩已不再放牛，
也不再是小孩，他是追隨夢想
的遊子，他在東京。93.04.05.
◎三十自述◎

建築
Architecture

建築是旅途中最動人的元素，特別是那些獨一無二的造型、構造、材料、風格，不論雄偉或婉約、精緻或粗獷，都有令人感動的地方……

Architecture is the most moving element of the journey, especially those unique shapes, structures, materials, and styles, whether majestic or graceful, delicate or rough, there are always moving places to touch emotion.......

Castle house stand over Mountain
Edinburgh 2006.02.19
Brodick Castle
Scottland . isle of Arran

View from Royal Musium. Edinburgh.
2006.02.19

A unic Castle. Edinburgh, Scotland.
This is the last weekend for my visiting.
Cloudy day is just like the arrival day.
Mount-Saint-Michel.
France.
Brodick Castle.
built by Celts.
3000 ~ 1600 BC. on the way to Bath.
Uk.

Meeting with Charles Rennie Mackintosh
in the Glasgow school of Art. Last day of
Journey in UK. 2006.04.08
In Slovenia Portorož
Whitepark Bay. Northern Ireland
2005.07.26
Fountainbleau France
THAMES FLOOD BARRIER
London Thames Barrier Park

Castel by River Danube.
A house built with rocks.
2001.09.14
The home of Peter Rabbit.
Hill Top.
District.
2012.09.07
1999.09.25

2013.04.20
Castello Sforzesco, Milano.
威尼斯、聖馬可廣場。鐘塔。2013.04.21.
2013.04.23

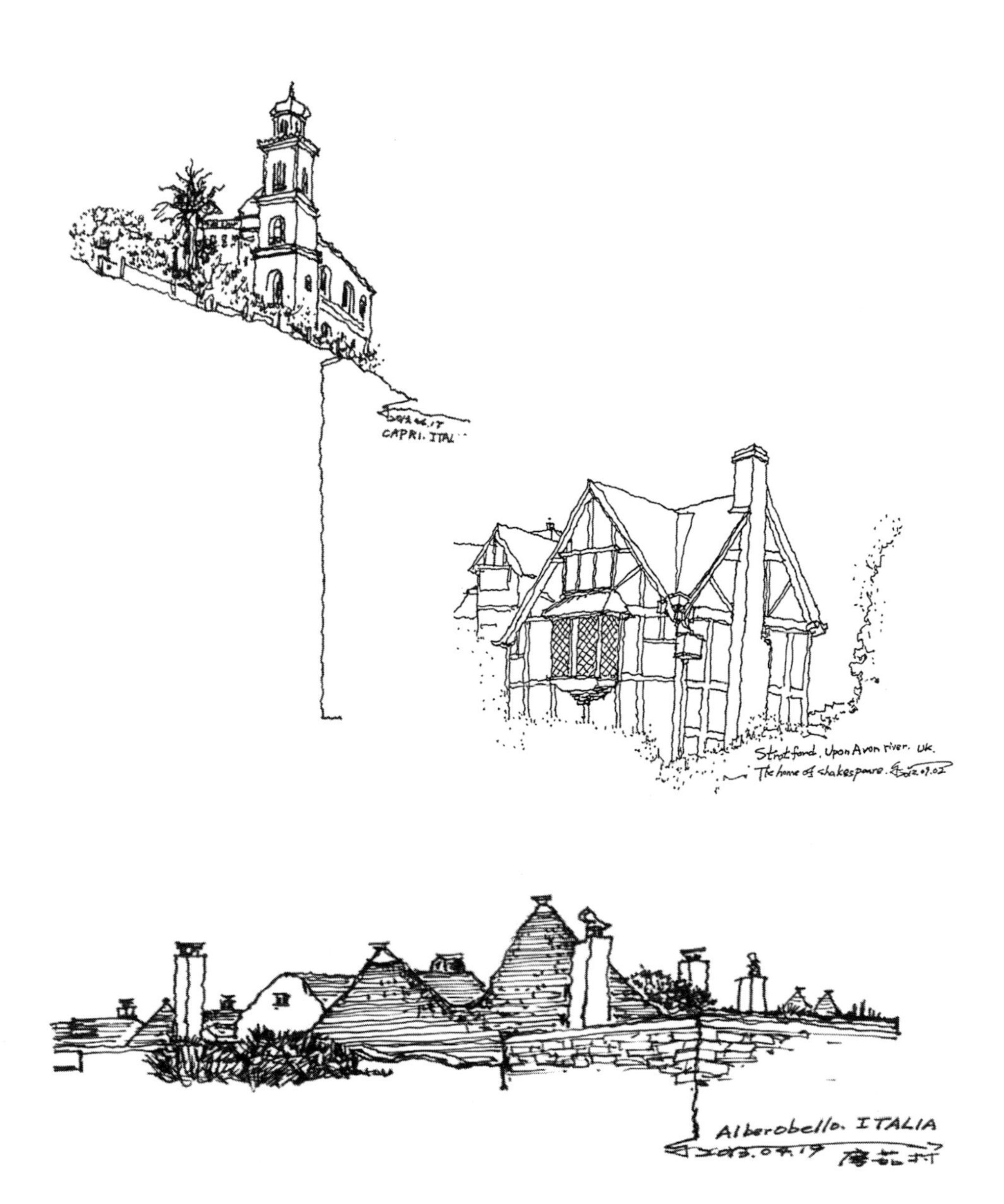
CAPRI. ITAL
Stratford. Upon Avon river. UK.
The home of shakespeare.
Alberobello. ITALIA

San Gimighano
Florence farview. from hill
The Lake and Bridge in Blenheim Palace
Waiting for oxford. Uk.
Cold Spring in

2013.04.18. St. Andrea Cathedral
AMALFI. ITALY.
Bridge of Firenze.
San Gimignano

Siena. Toscana. Italy.
2013.04.26. ROMA.
SAN GIMIGNANO

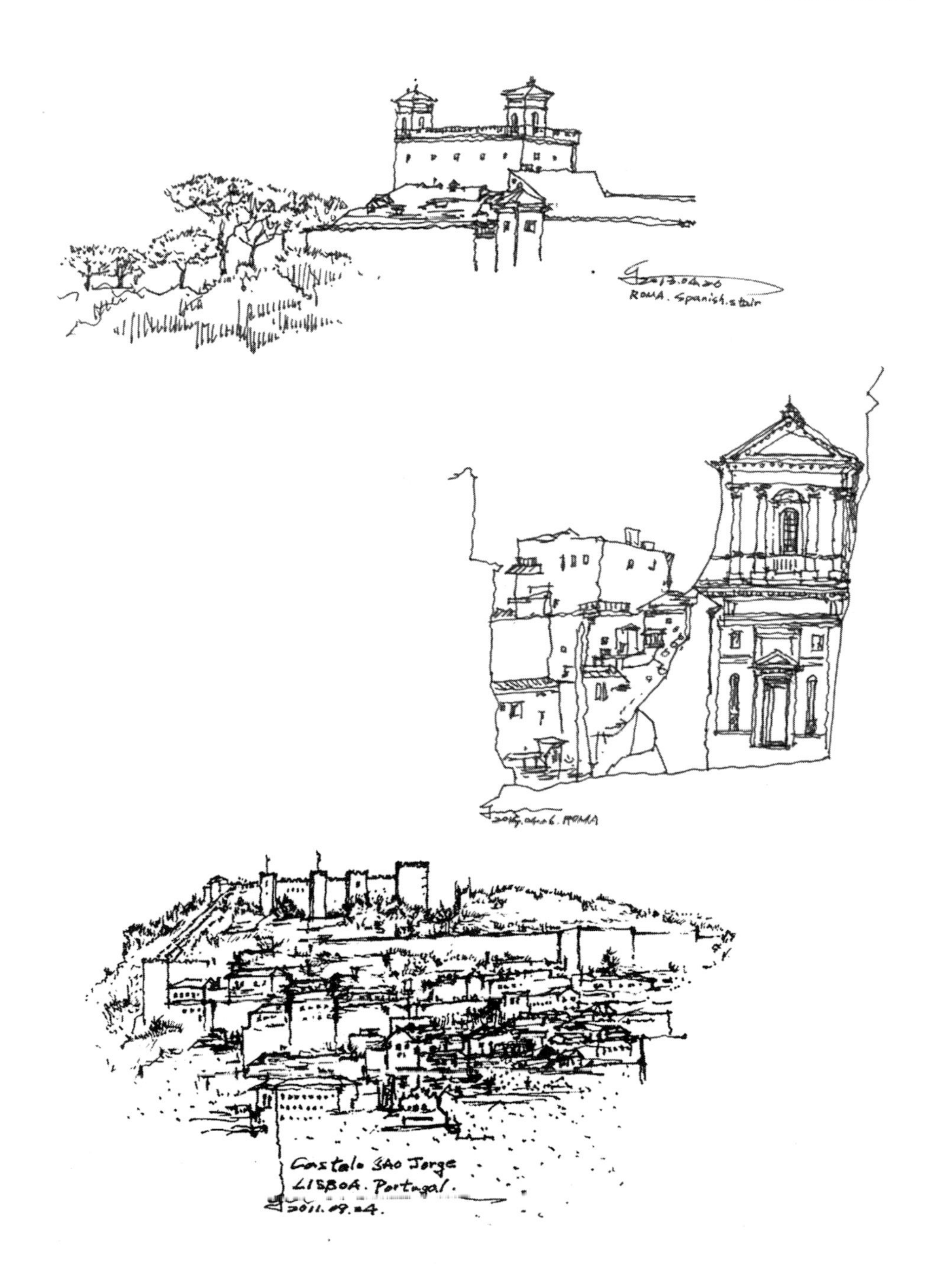
ROMA. Spanish.stair
Castelo SAO Jorge
LISBOA. Portugal.
2011.09.24.

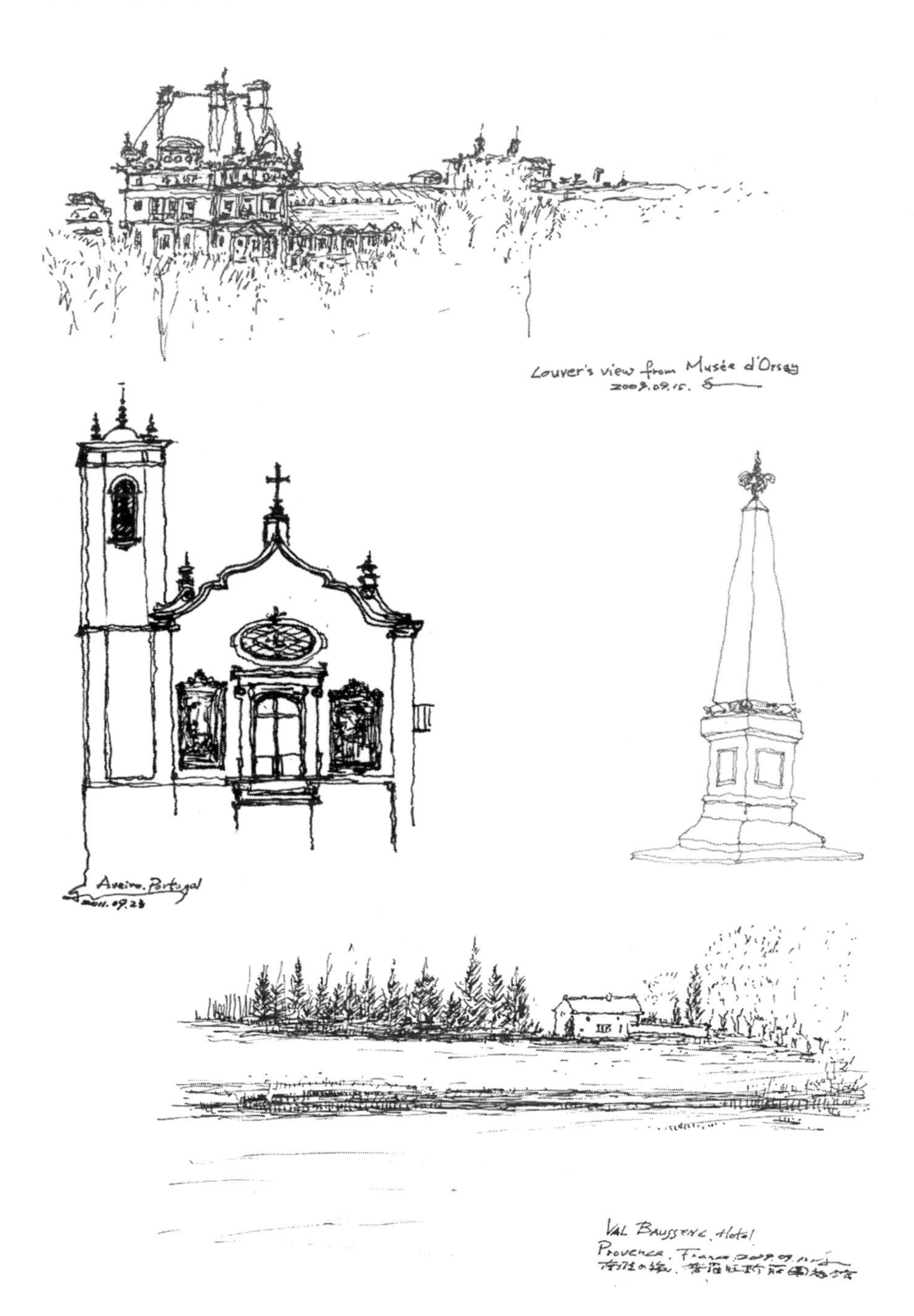
Louver's view from Musée d'Orsay
Aveiro, Portugal
2011.09.23
VAL BAUSSENC, Hotel
Provence, France

Wroclaw. Poland
STIRLING. CASTLE
Tour.
3rd.visit. Gaudi.
Sagrada Familla,
Barcelona. Span.
Sintra. Palace's Stack.

Sunset Impress
in Hanuman-dhoka
Kathmandu. Nepal.
2012.02.03.

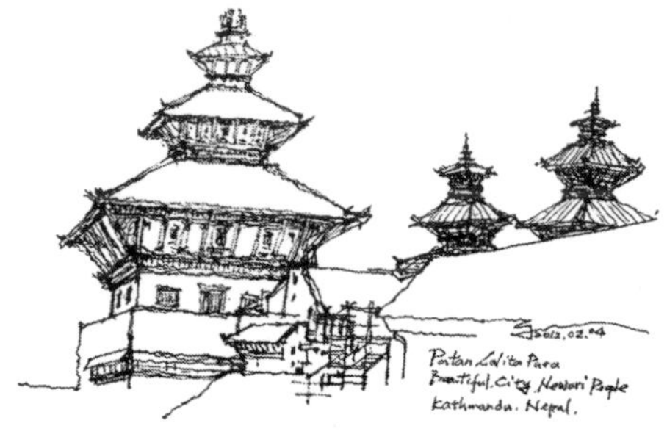
2012.02.04
Patan Lalita Para
Beautiful. City Newari People
Kathmandu. Nepal.

Bhaktapur City
Kathmandu Nepal.
2012.02.05

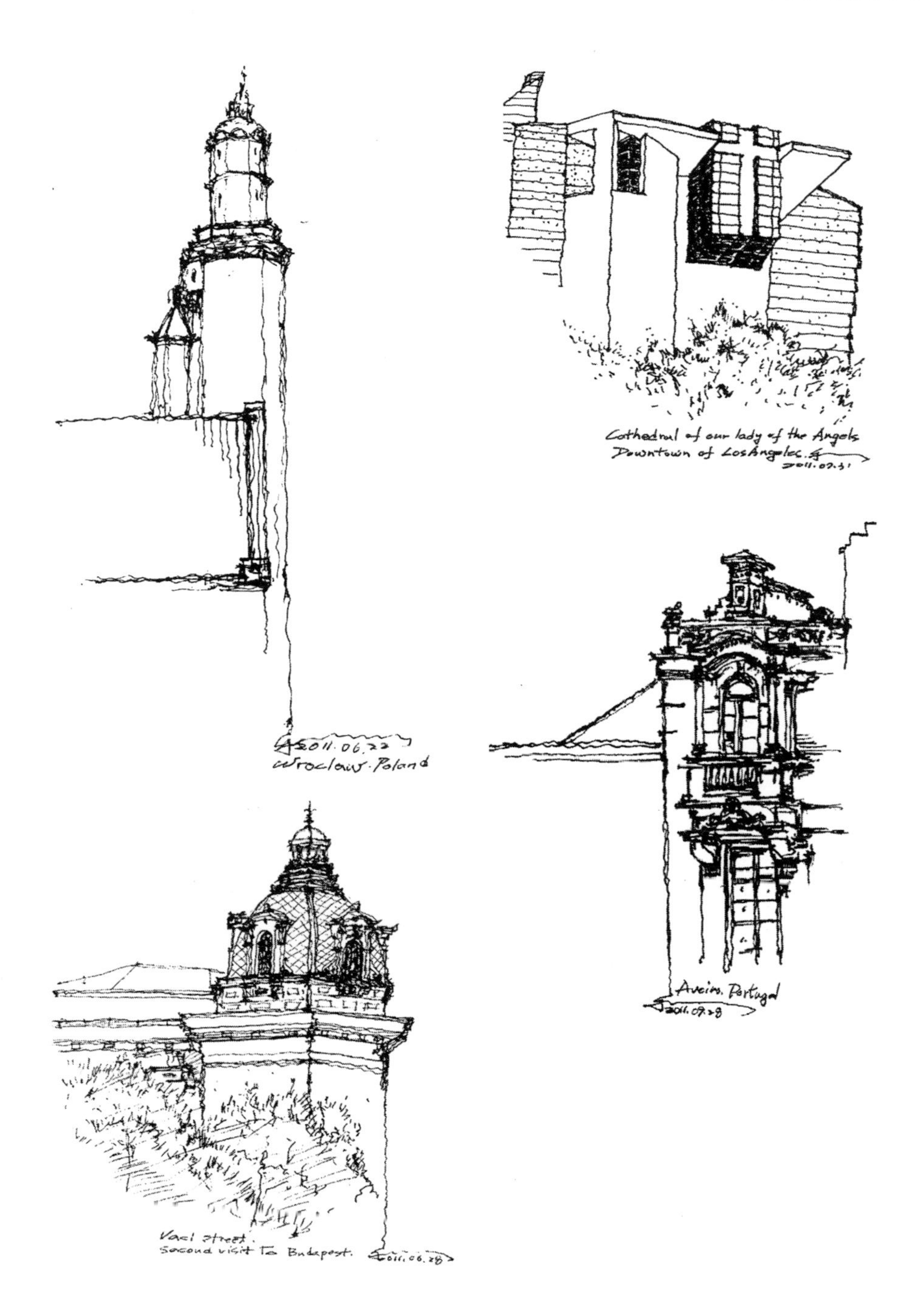
2011.06.22
Wroclaw·Poland
Cathedral of our lady of the Angels
Downtown of LosAngeles.
2011.07.31
Aveiro. Portugal
2011.07.28
Vaci street.
Second visit to Budapest.
2011.06.28

Belfast. street coner. 2005.09.28

Prague

Vienna. 2011.06

St. Giles', The high kirk of Edinburgh.
2006.02.19

Sevilla. Spain
Portugal. Sintra Palace
2002.12.29
KÖLN
Sigh. Bridge. Trinity Hall
Cambridge. England
2012.07.04

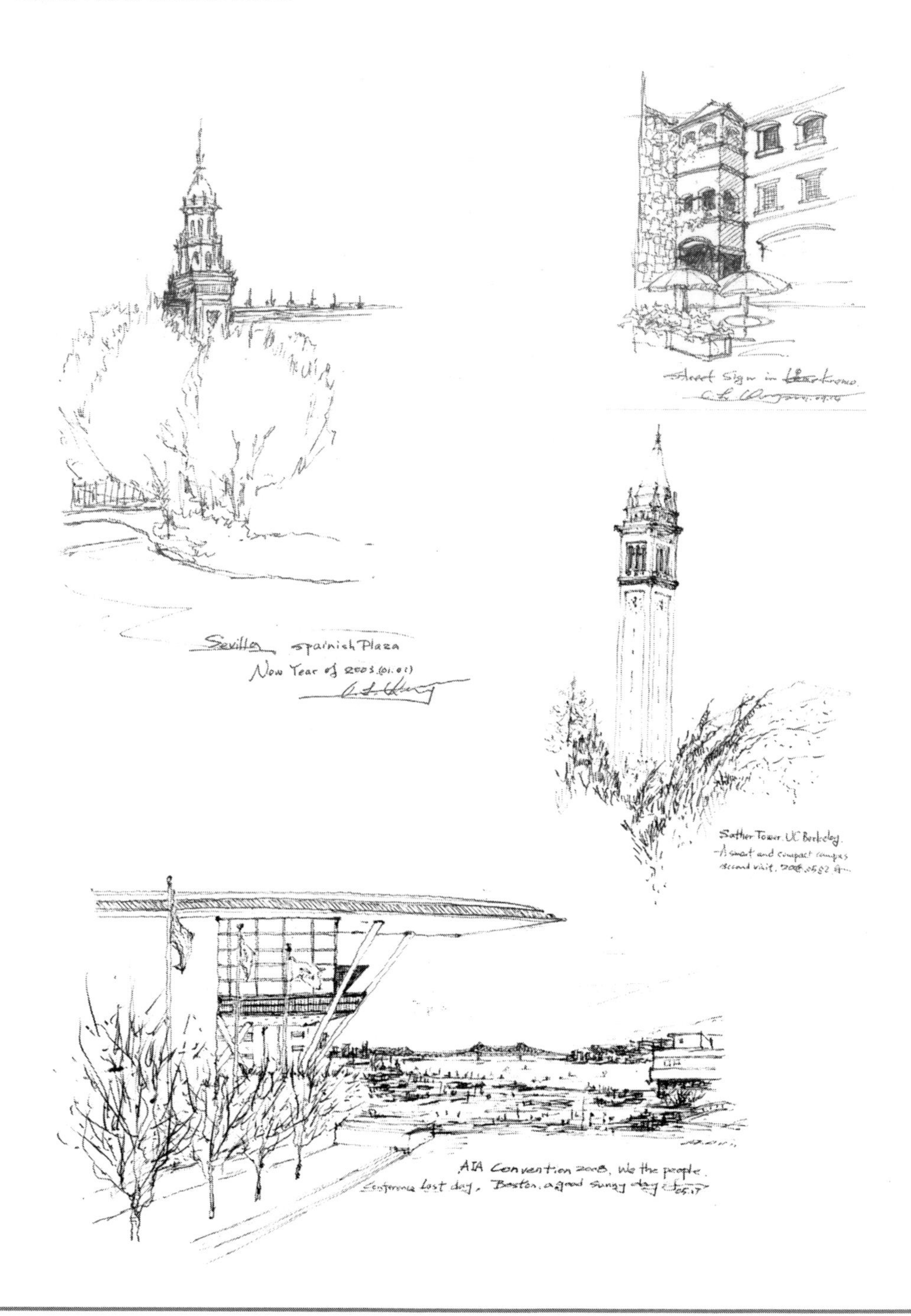
Sevilla spainish Plaza
Sather Tower. UC Berkeley.
AIA Convention 2008, We the people.
Conference last day, Boston, a good sunny day

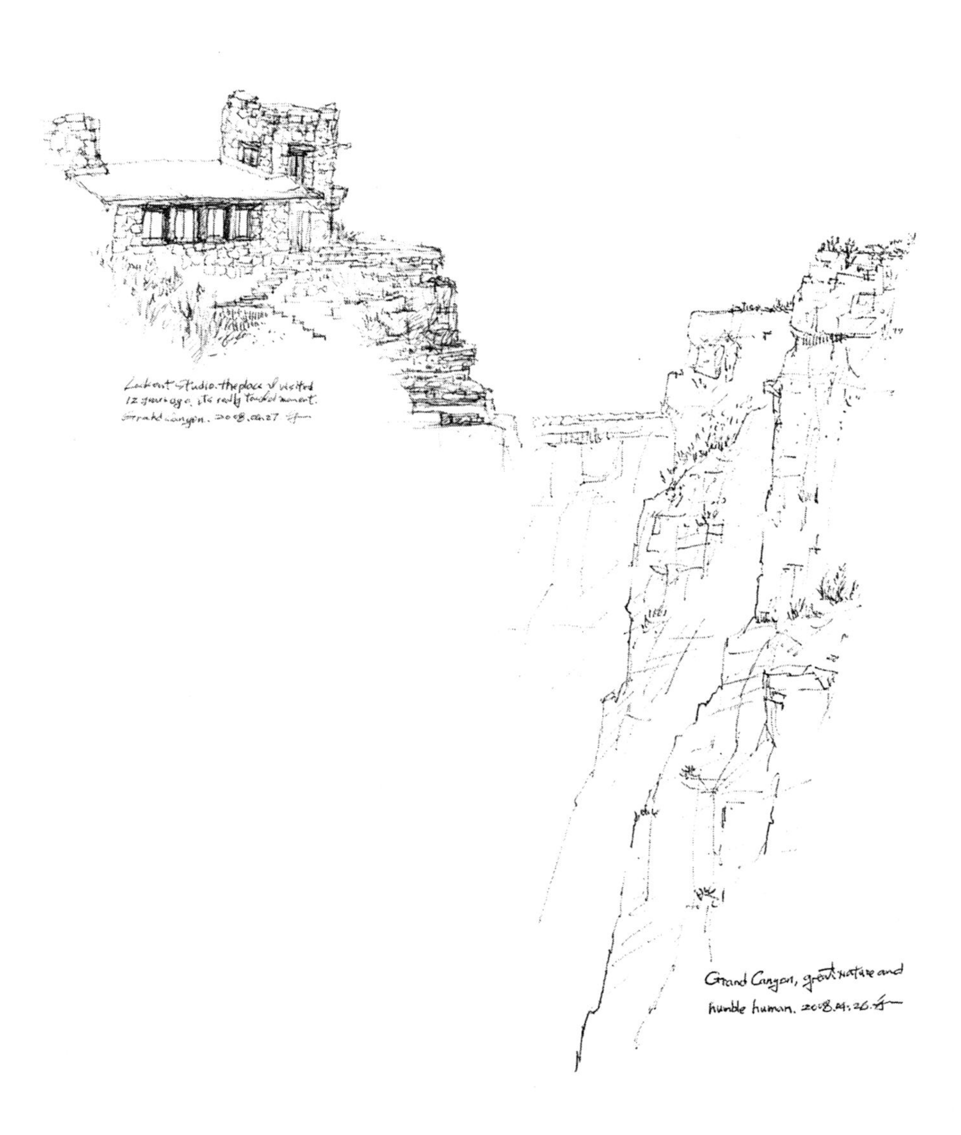
Lookout Studio. the place I visited
12 years ago, its really touched moment.
Grand Canyon. 2008.04.27
Grand Canyon, great nature and
humble human. 2008.04.26.

Spruce tree House
Cliff Palace,
magic and wonder for
Ancestral Puebloan people.

Cliff Palace, Mesa Verde
complex structure of Village
Navajo Cliff dwelling. Canyon de Chelly.
Valley visiting
Pueblo Bonito, Chaco Culture
NATL Historical Park New Mexico

Lookout Studio
The Grand Canyon
1996.07.01
The Lookout
KOLB STUDIO
Grand Canyon USA
2015.07.09
Grand Canyon National Park
West Rim. Sky Walk.
2014.09.16

好客的哈薩克牧人家
那拉提夏牧場
天空草原
2012.07.18
草坡上的氈房
2012.07.9
草原牧人的氈房
2012.06.14

北疆賽里木湖的清晨 2012.05.16
天鵝的約会.

北疆之旅.喀纳斯
禾木村.河边的木屋
2012.07.12

北疆之旅.布尔津 禾木村
图瓦人的家 2012.07.12

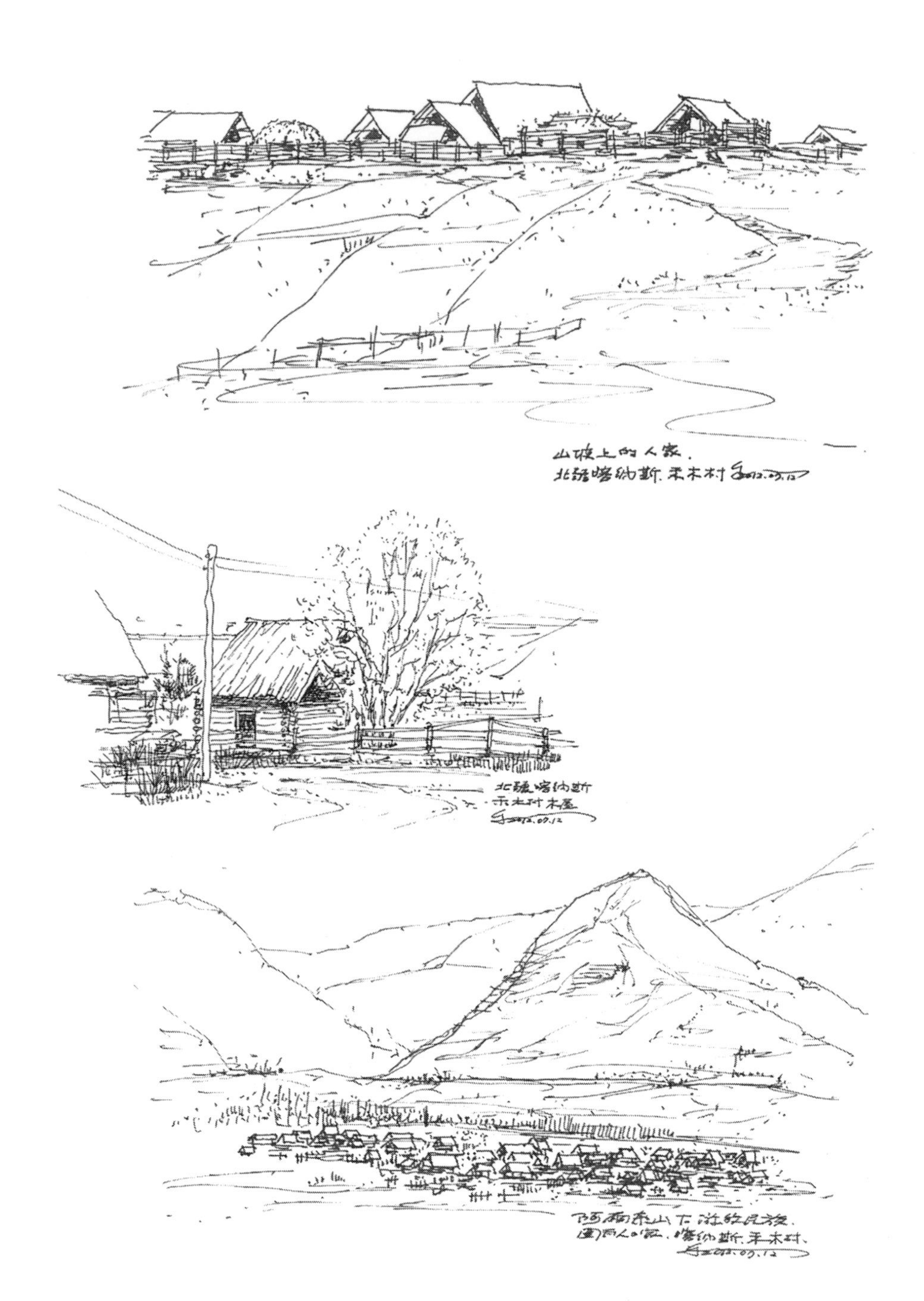
山坡上的人家.
北疆喀納斯. 禾木村 2012.07.12
北疆喀納斯
禾木村木屋
2012.07.12
阿爾泰山下游牧民族.
圖瓦人的家. 喀納斯. 禾木村.
2012.07.12

昭苏草原花海
山坡上草原牧人の家

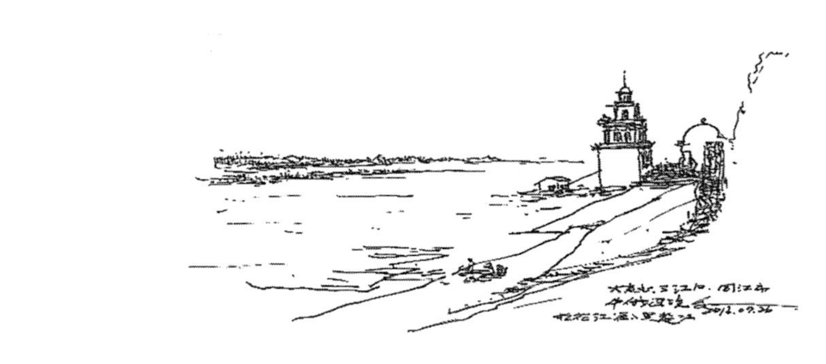

2013.08.02
北極村.漠河
2013.08.03

大東北中国漠河北極村
2013.08.02
中国極北国境
漠河北極村
北方人家

民族飯店

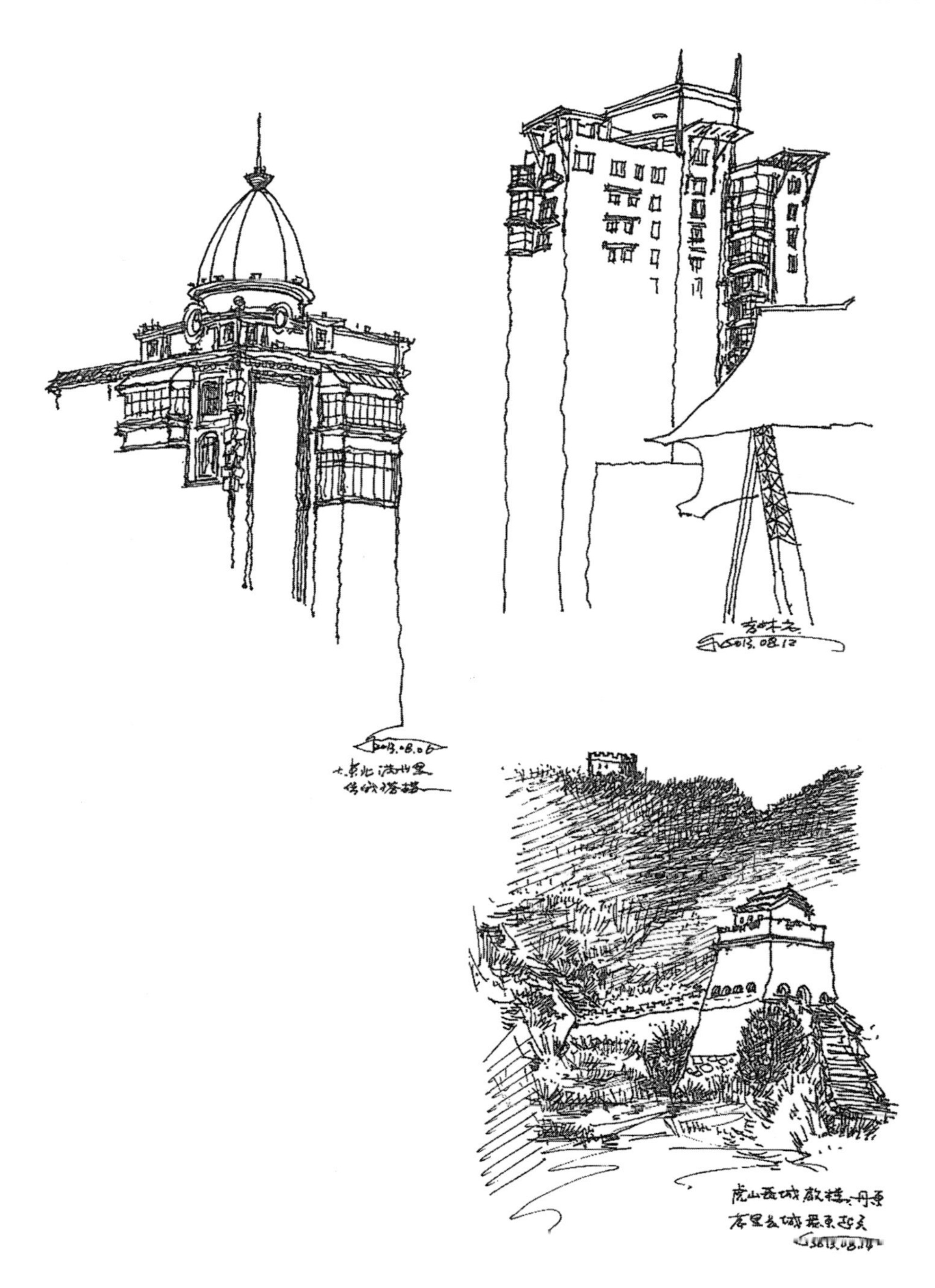
2013.08.12
2013.08.06
七.東北滿州里
俄式塔樓
虎山長城敵樓、丹東
萬里長城最東起点

拉薩.布達拉宮
2017.07.22 西藏之旅
雍布拉康.西藏
2017.07.16
江孜白居寺/西藏

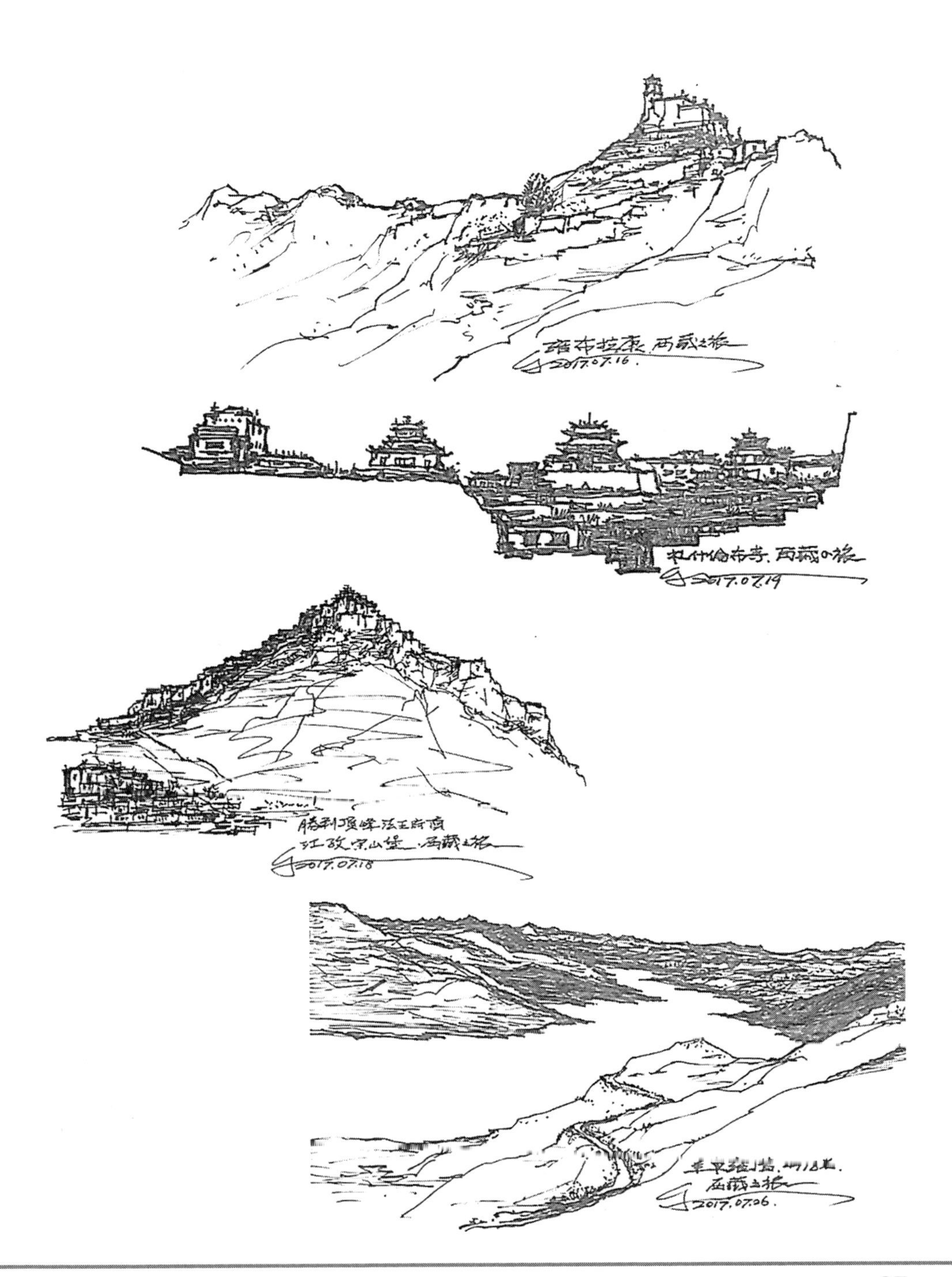
雍布拉康.西藏之旅
2017.07.16.
扎什伦布寺.西藏之旅
2017.07.19
勝利頂峰法王府頂
江孜宗山堡.西藏之旅
2017.07.18
西藏之旅
2017.07.26.

Machu picchu 2014.04.23

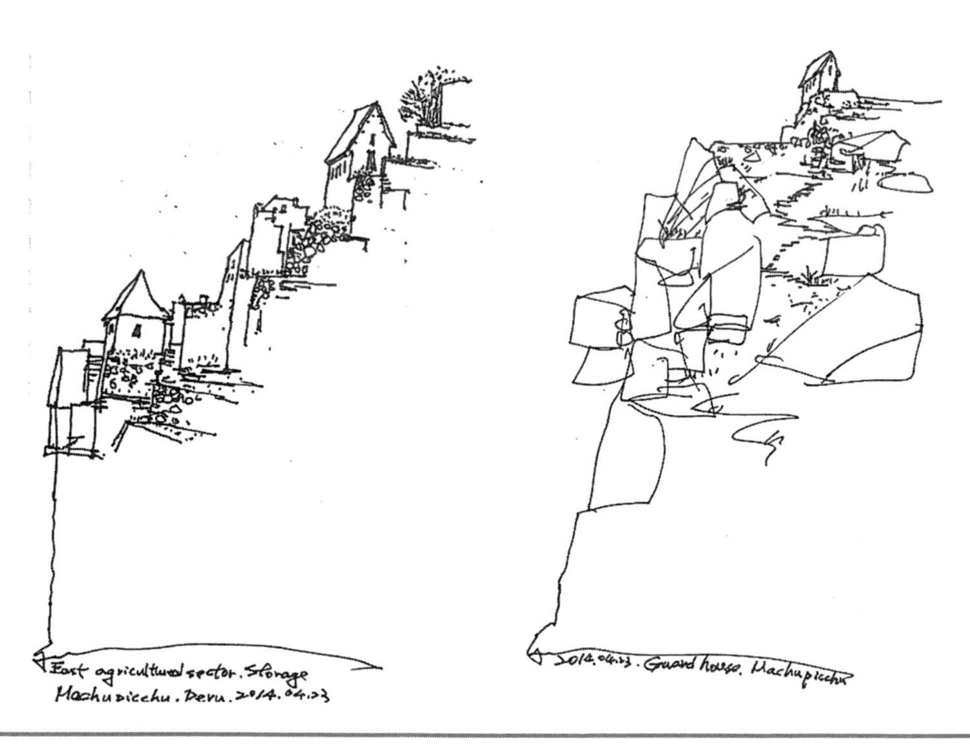
East agricultural sector. Storage
Machu picchu. Peru. 2014.04.23
2014.04.23. Guard house. Machupicchu

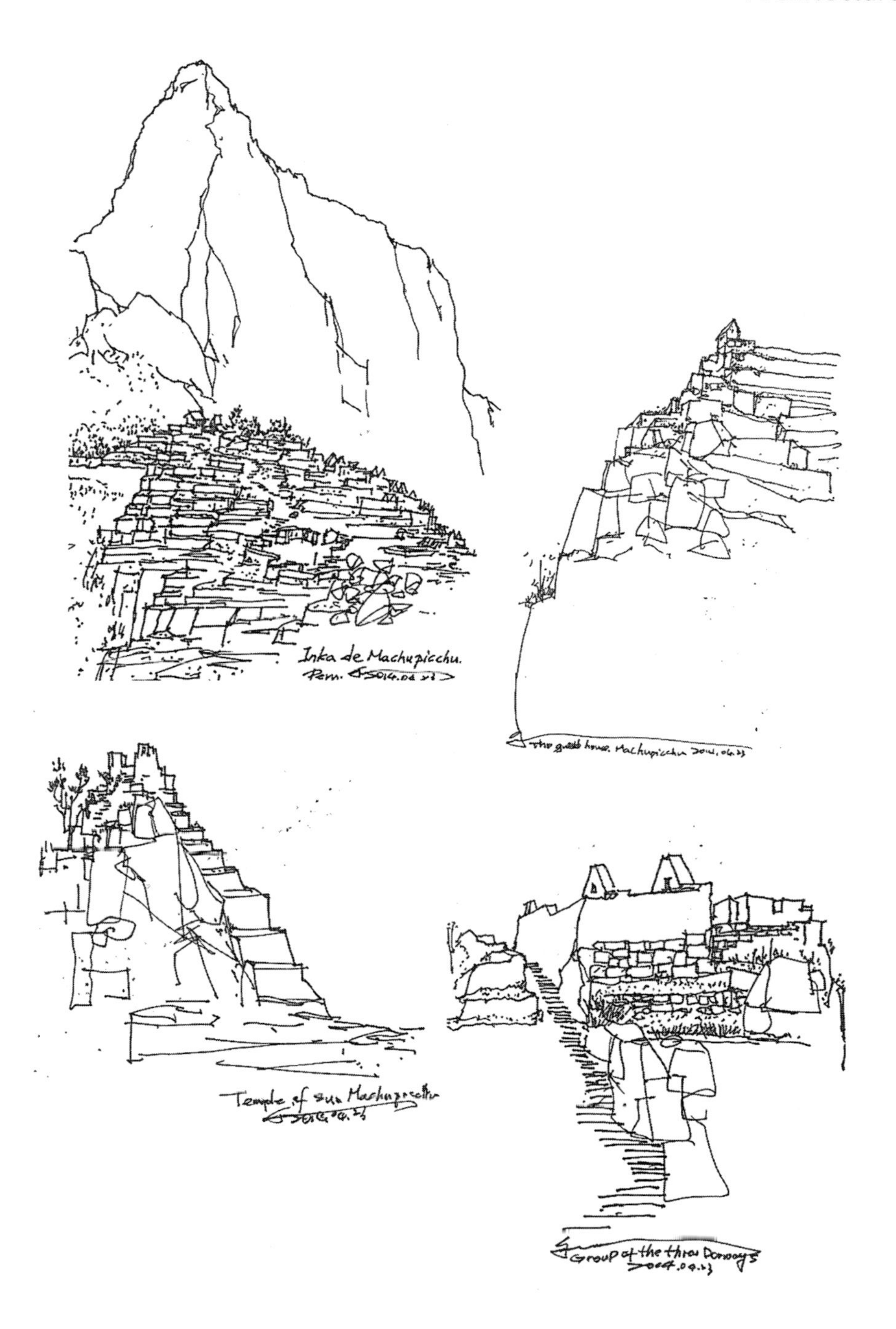
Inka de Machupicchu.
Peru.
the guest house. Machupicchu
Temple of sun
Group of the

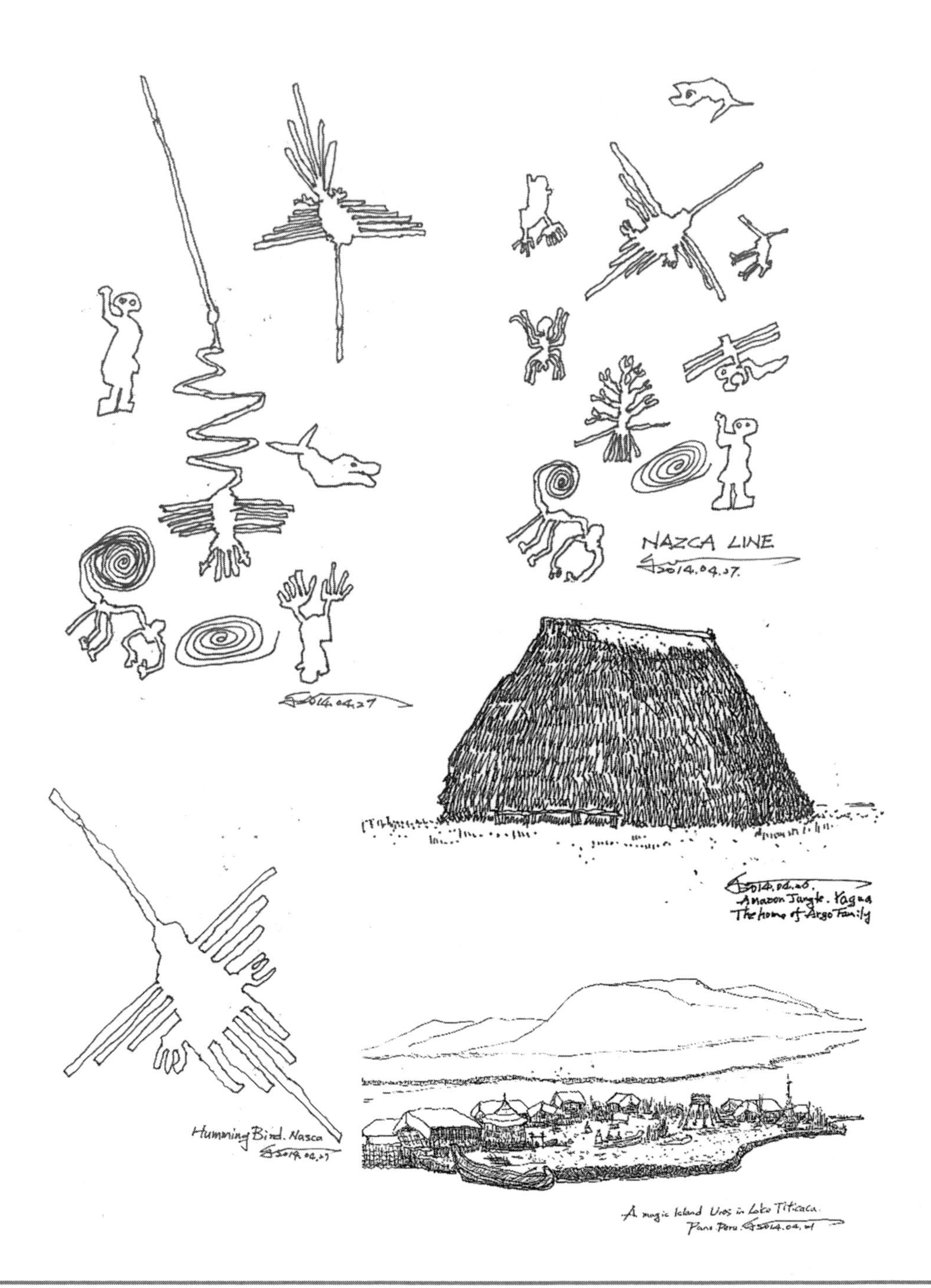
NAZCA LINE
2014.04.27.
2014.04.27
Amazon Jungle. Yagua
The home of Argo Family
Humming Bird. Nasca
A magic Island Uros in Lake Titicaca.
Puno Peru.

SACRER VALLEY
A magic Island Uros in Lake
Puno. Peru

ARANWA CAPILLA CHAPEL. PERU
2014.04.24.
Arequipa Church.
Peru. 2014.04.20
Larco Museo. Lima
2014.04.17

image of Chicago.

Golden Gate Bridge
San Francisco. CA. trip
Antiques Center
Danish Village. Way to Fresno
Travel. California. USA
2007.04.04
Campus CalPoly Pomona CA California USA
Administration Building
Campus of CalPoly Pomona. LA

Hattingen. German
Altstadtrundgang
Visit Dusseldorf. Germany

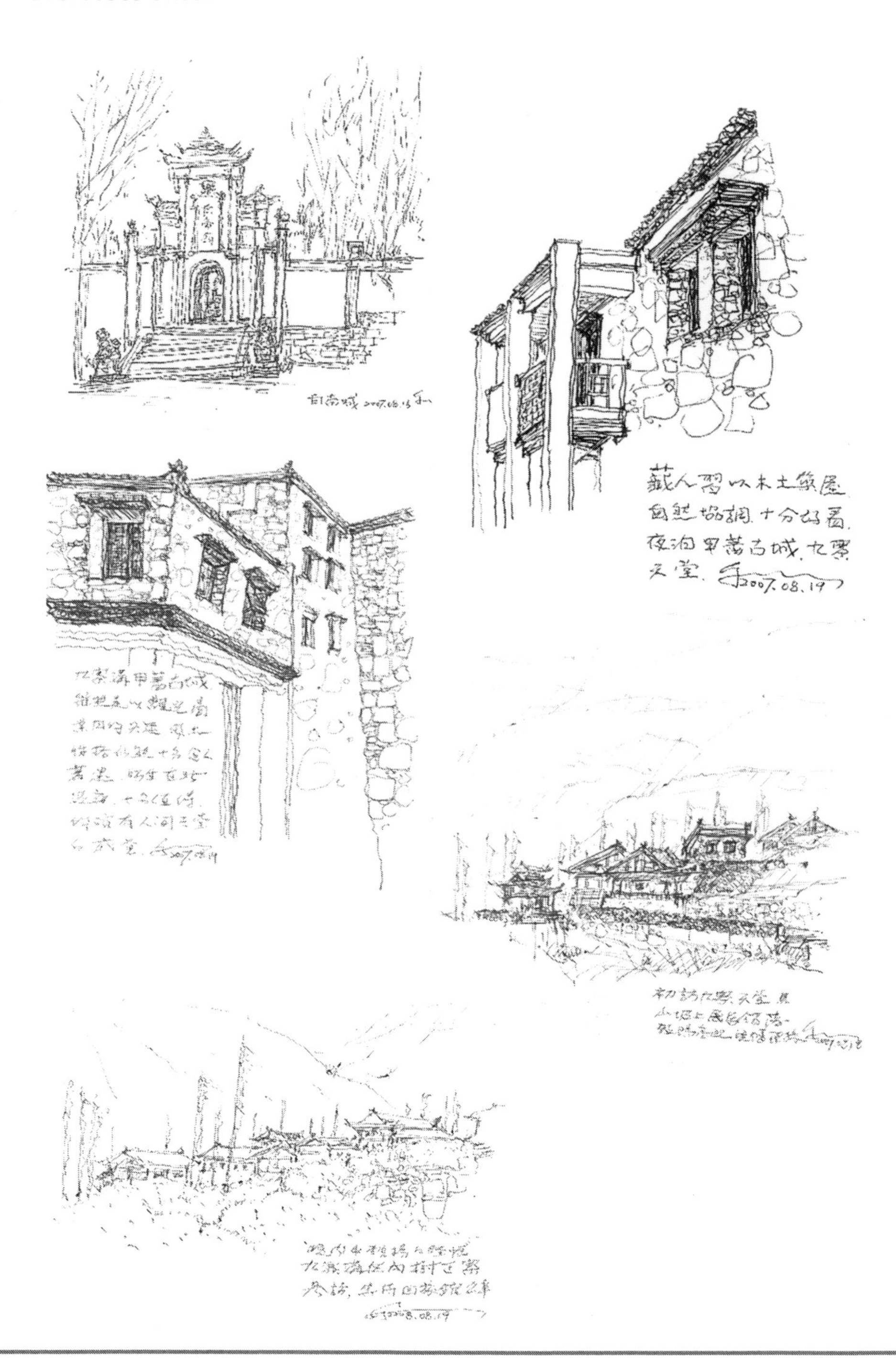
藏人習以木土築屋
自然協調．十分好看．
夜泊甲蕃古城．九寨
天堂．2007.08.19

2016.8.21 Split
Croatia.
2016.08.21 Split.
Croatia.
2016.8.22 Sucuraj
Croatia. Hvar Island
Waiting for ferry in a small harbor

2016.08.21. Split.
Croatia
2016.08.22. Adriatic Sea. Hvar Island. Croatia
2016.08.22
Stari Grad. Croatia

2016.08.20 Dubrovnik
Croatia
2016.08.23
Dubrovnik, Croatia
2016.08.24. Dubrovnik
Croatia

2016.08.27 Dubrovnik
Croatia. Adriatic Sea

2016.09.01. Kosice. slovania

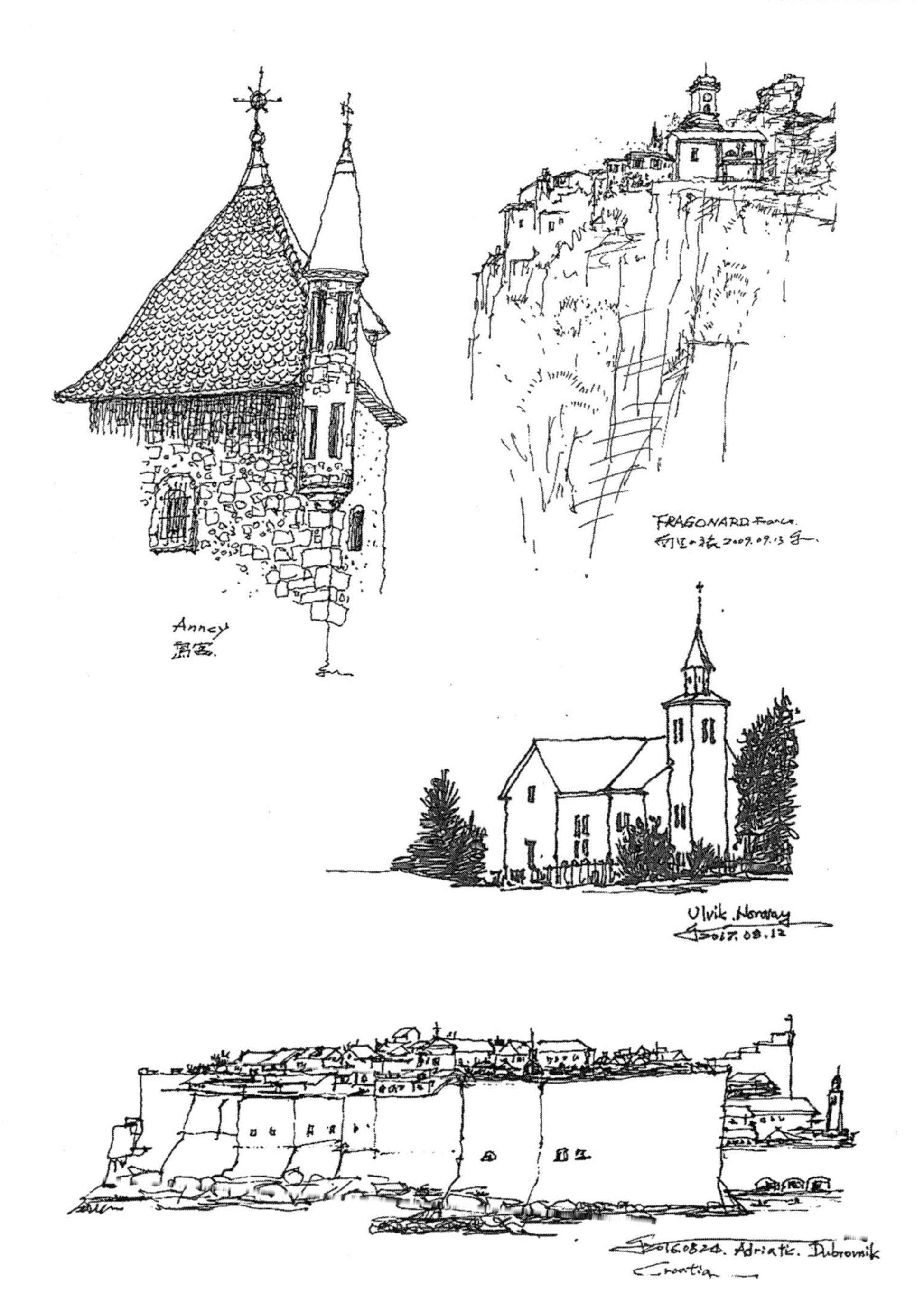
Annecy
FRAGONARD France.
Ulvik .Norway
2017.08.12
2016.08.24. Adriatic. Dubrovnik
Croatia

impression of Copenhagen
Denmark
Kosice
Slovakia
Kristiansand
Norway

2016.08.18. Bled
2016.08.17. Graz. Austrian.
2016.08.22 Sucuraj
Waiting for ferry in a small harbor

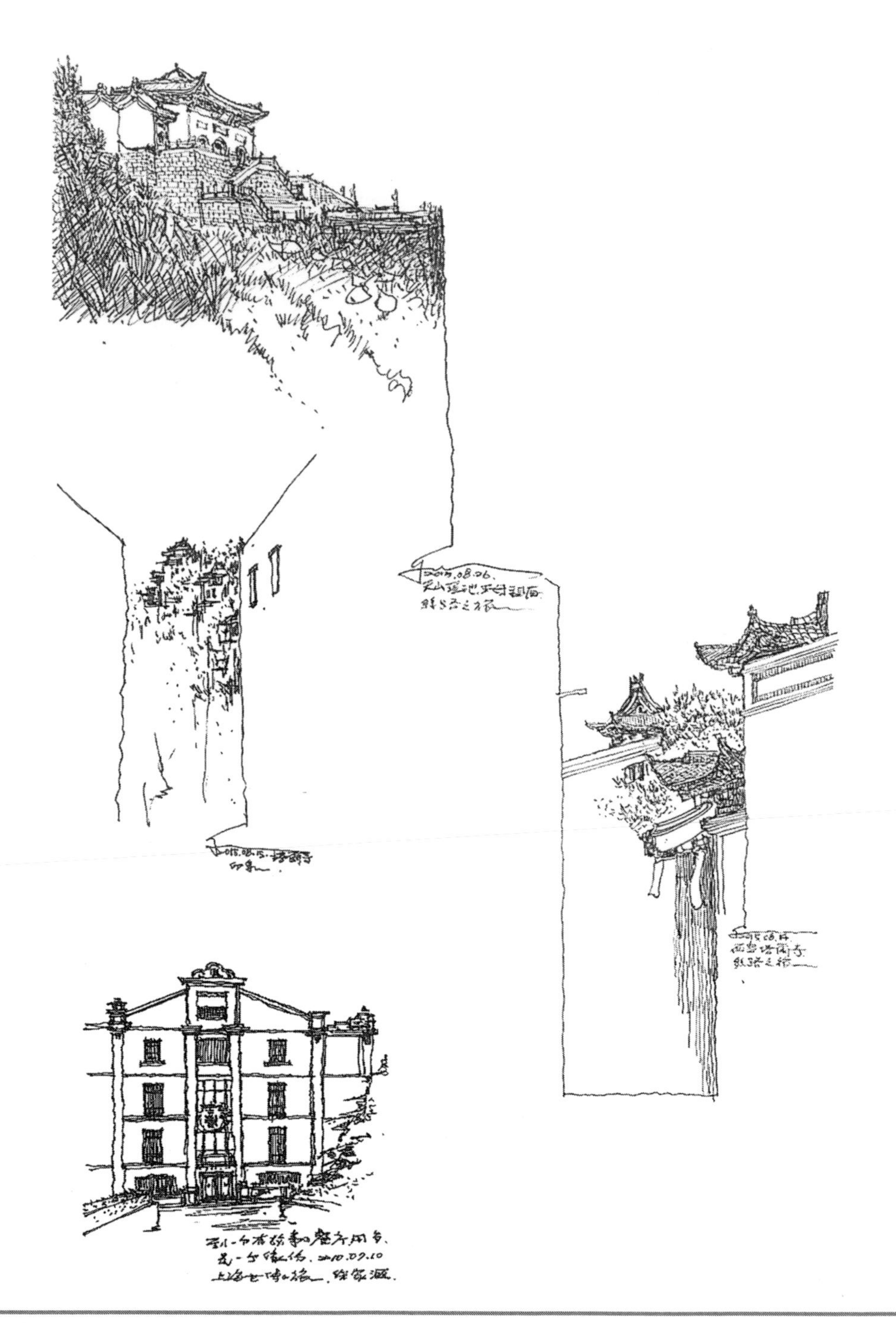

Unnamed Church on main street
North Bridge of Concord

Town Hall of concord.
The old Manse Boathouse
Tree above the river and boat house.
Under north Bridge. Concord, Boston

The Crystal Cathedral
by Philip Johnson in Orange, California. US.
Tower of New Hope. Crystal Cathedral
by Richard Neutra in Orange. LA. CA. 2008.05.29.
Train Station West Concord. 2008.05.23

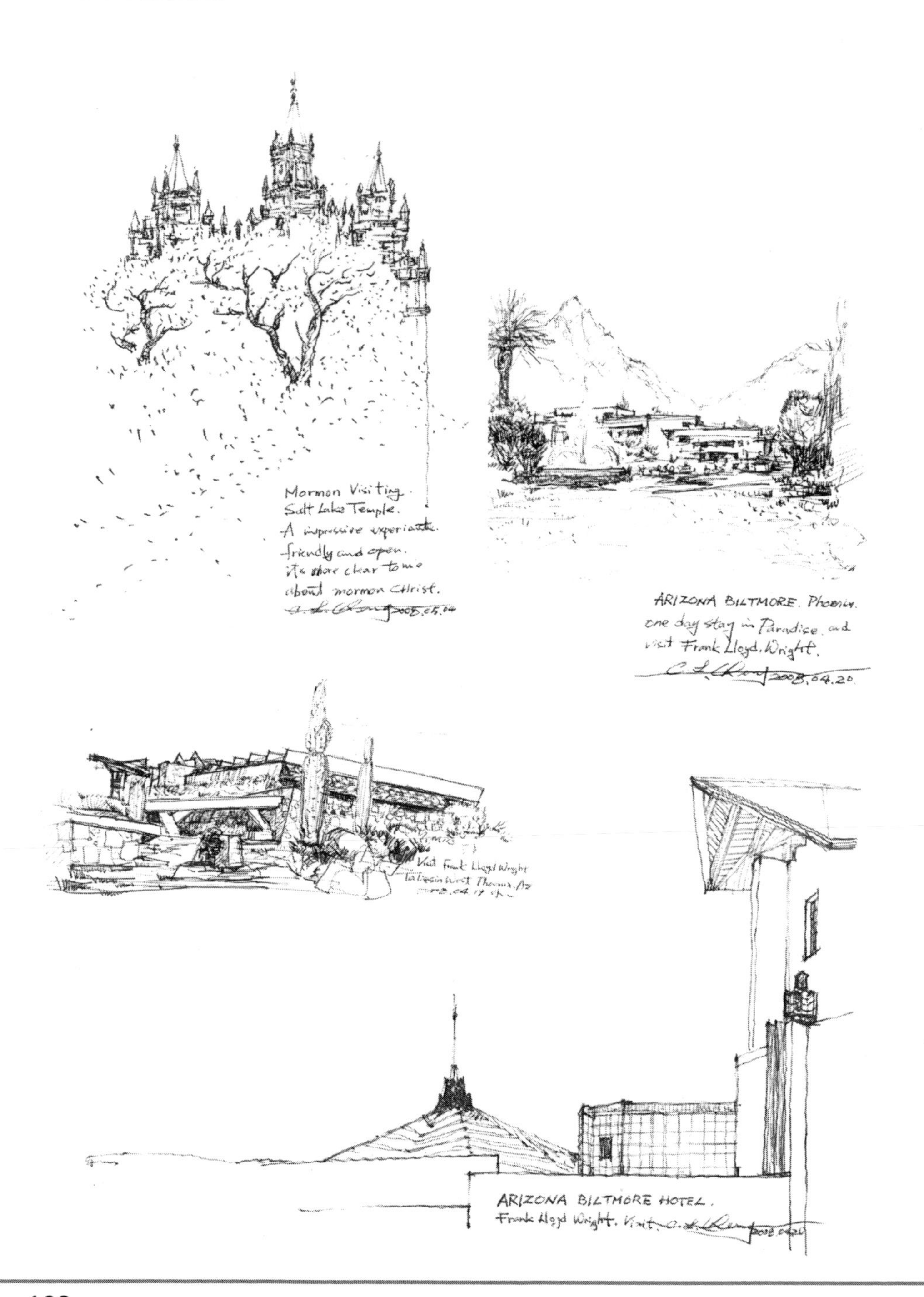
Mormon Visiting
Salt Lake Temple.
A impressive experiance.
friendly and open.
its more clear to me
about mormon Christ.
ARIZONA BILTMORE. Phoenix.
one day stay in Paradise. and
visit Frank Lloyd. Wright.
2008.04.20.
Visit Frank Lloyd Wright
Taliesin West Phoenix. Az
ARIZONA BILTMORE HOTEL.
Frank Lloyd Wright. Visit.

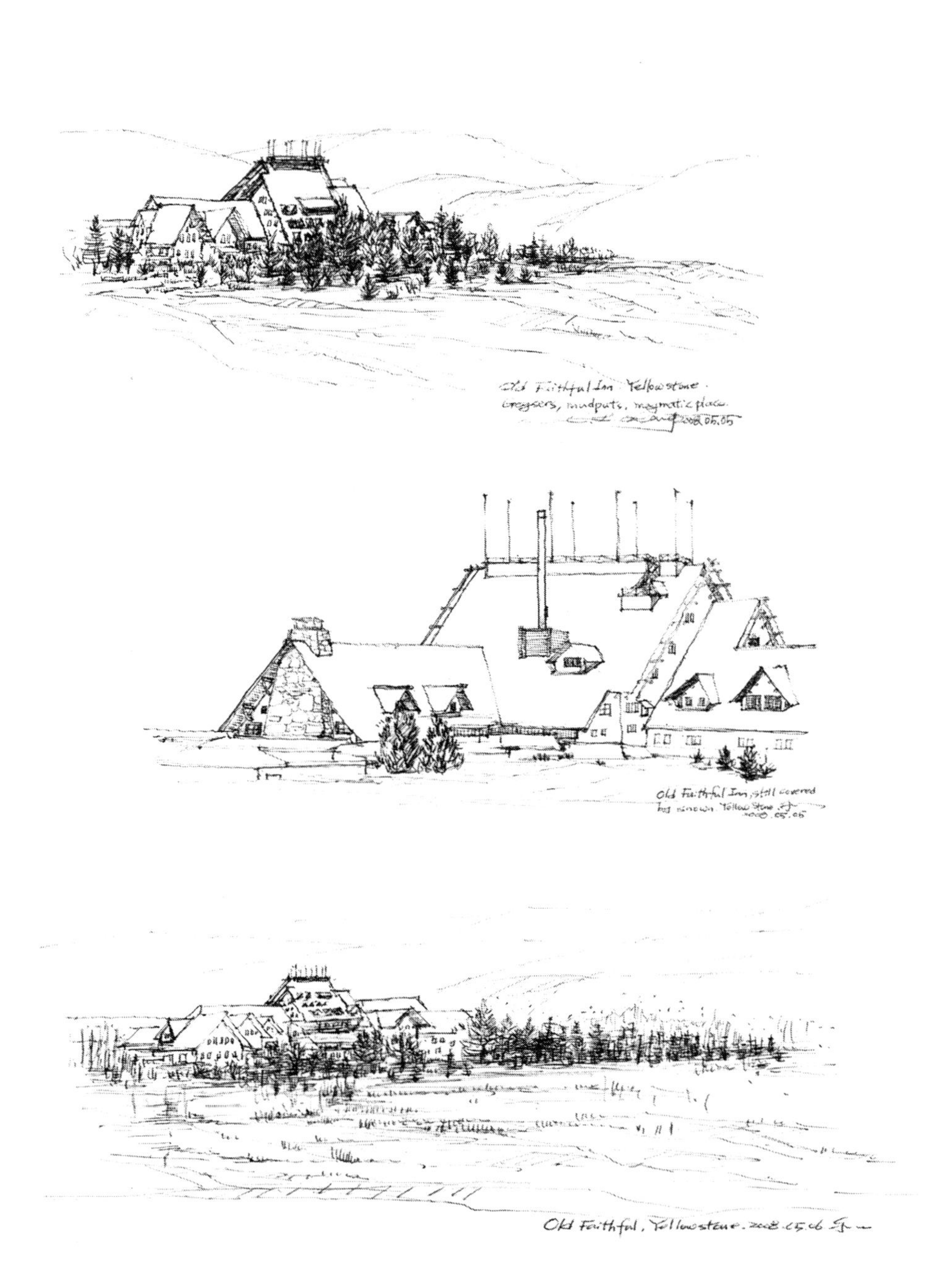
Faithful Inn Yellowstone.
mudpots, magmatic place.
2008.05.05
Old Faithful Inn, still covered
by snow. Yellow Stone
2008.05.05
Old Faithful, Yellowstone. 2008.05.06

Gustavus Inn, a bountiful day. Alaska 2008.06.29
Cabin House in Gustavus. Alaska. 2008.06.29

An abandoned house in Gustavus.
Alaska. 2008.06.29.

The Statue of Liberty
New York
Washington Monument.

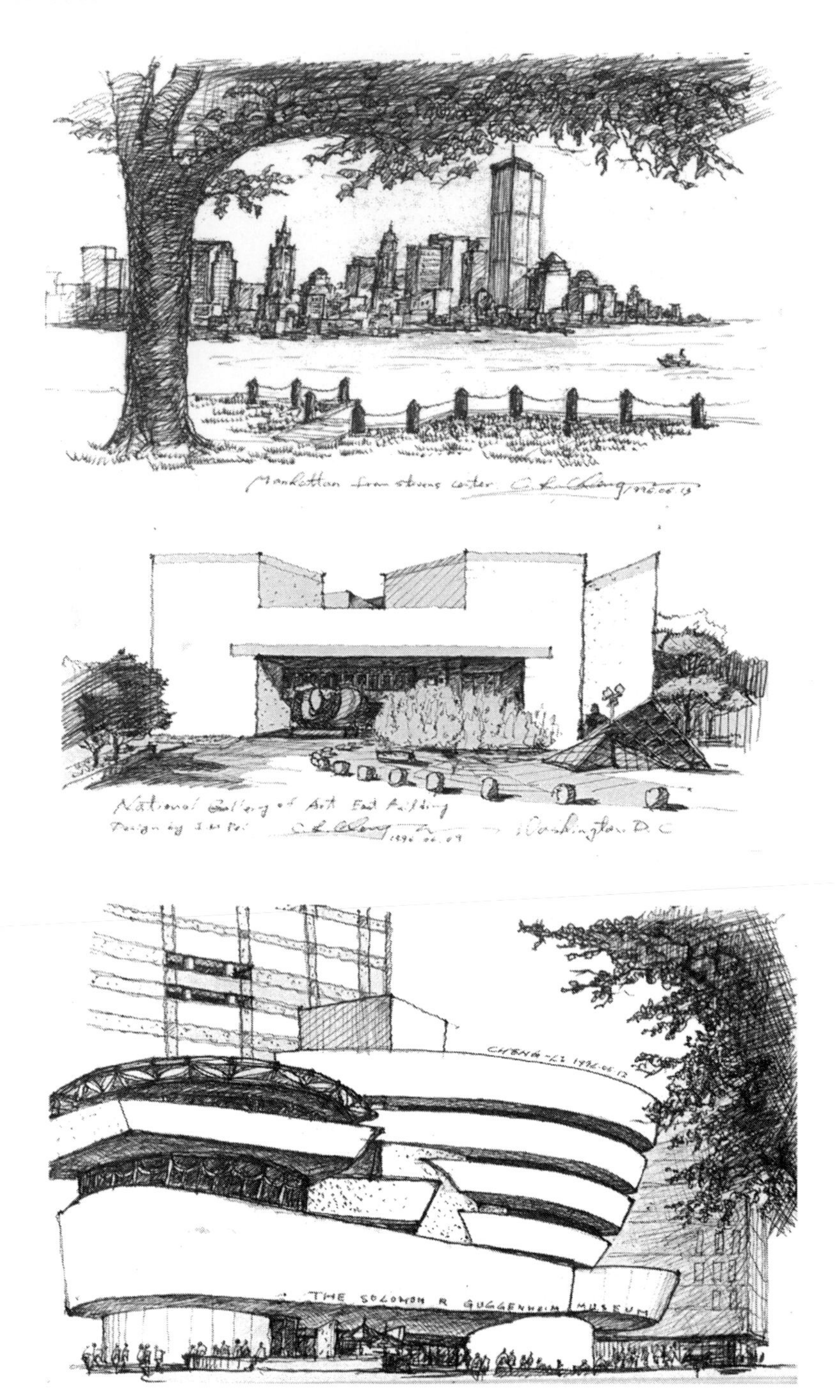
National Gallery of Art East Building
Washington D.C
THE SOLOMON R GUGGENHEIM MUSEUM

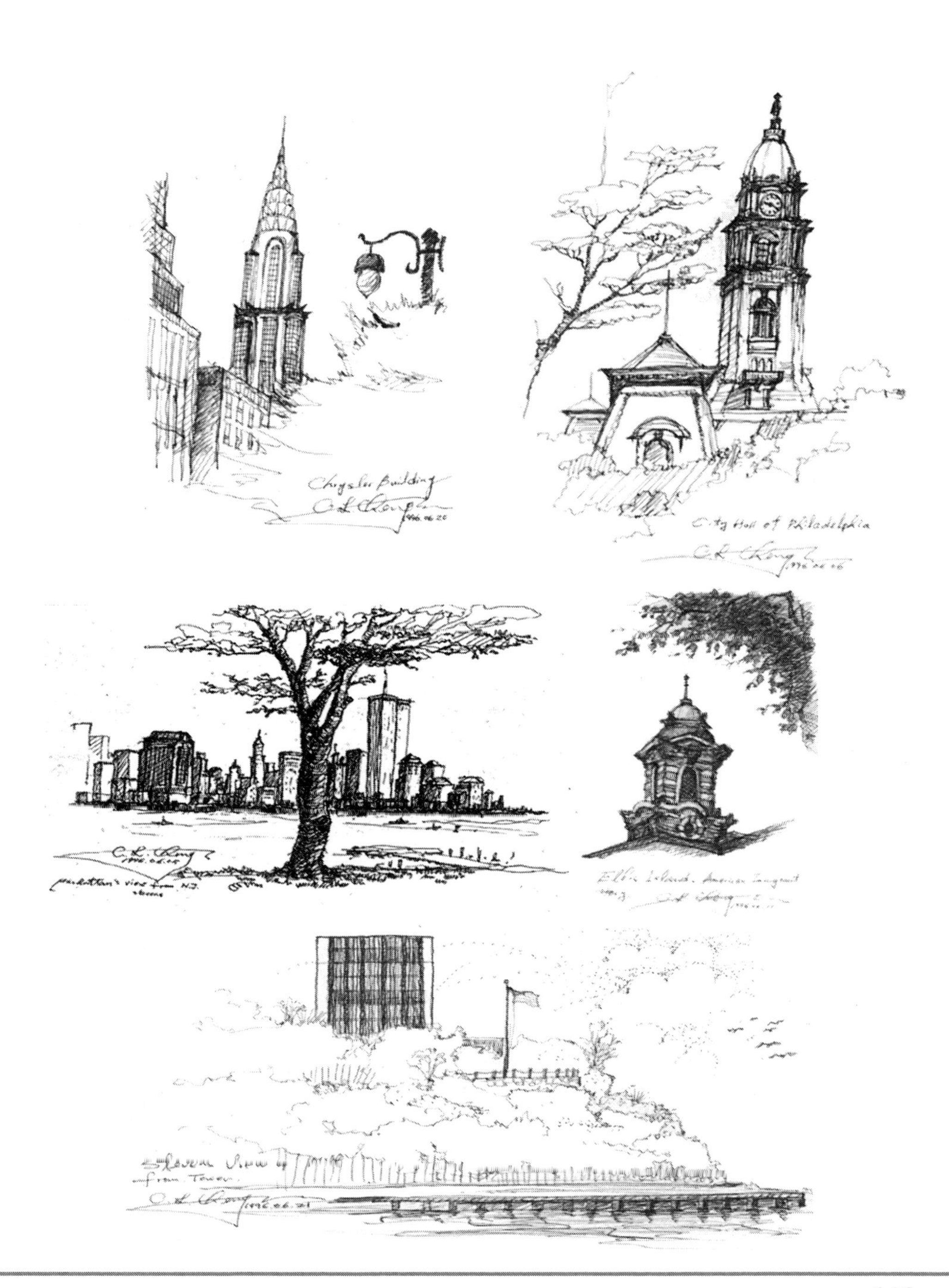
Chrysler Building
City Hall of Philadelphia

Detroit Renaissance Center

City Hall of Toronto.

United Nations Headquarter

Toronto City Hall's view from Sheraton

University of Stanford
1996.07.01
Stanford
1996.07.07
University of California Berkeley
1996.07.07

Hotel Cataratas. Iguasu
Brazil. 2000.09.16

Building in cliff. Dürnstein
Journey in river Danube.
Hill House
CABO DA ROCA
The end of Land and begining of Sea.

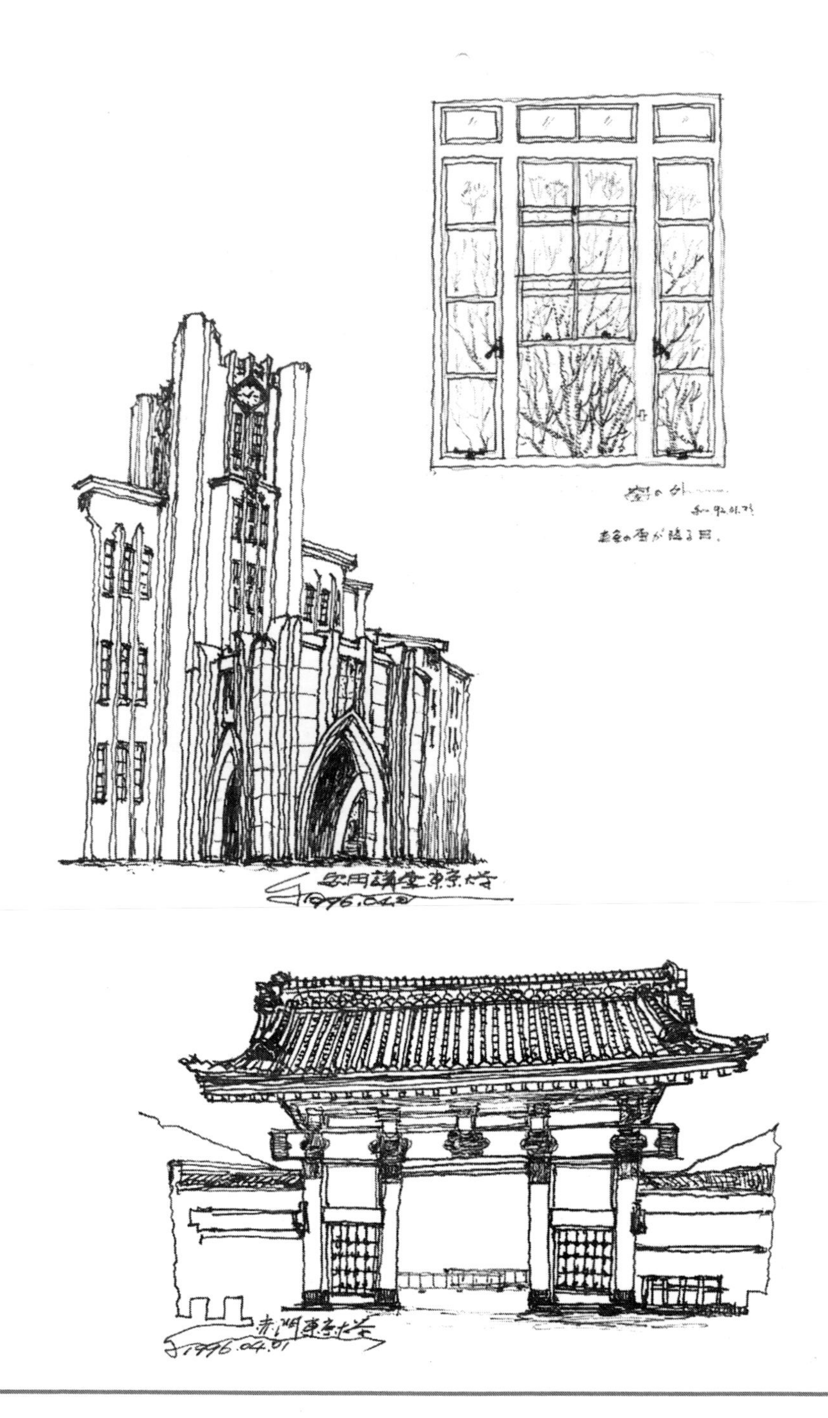
安田講堂 東京大学
赤門 東京大学
1996.04.01

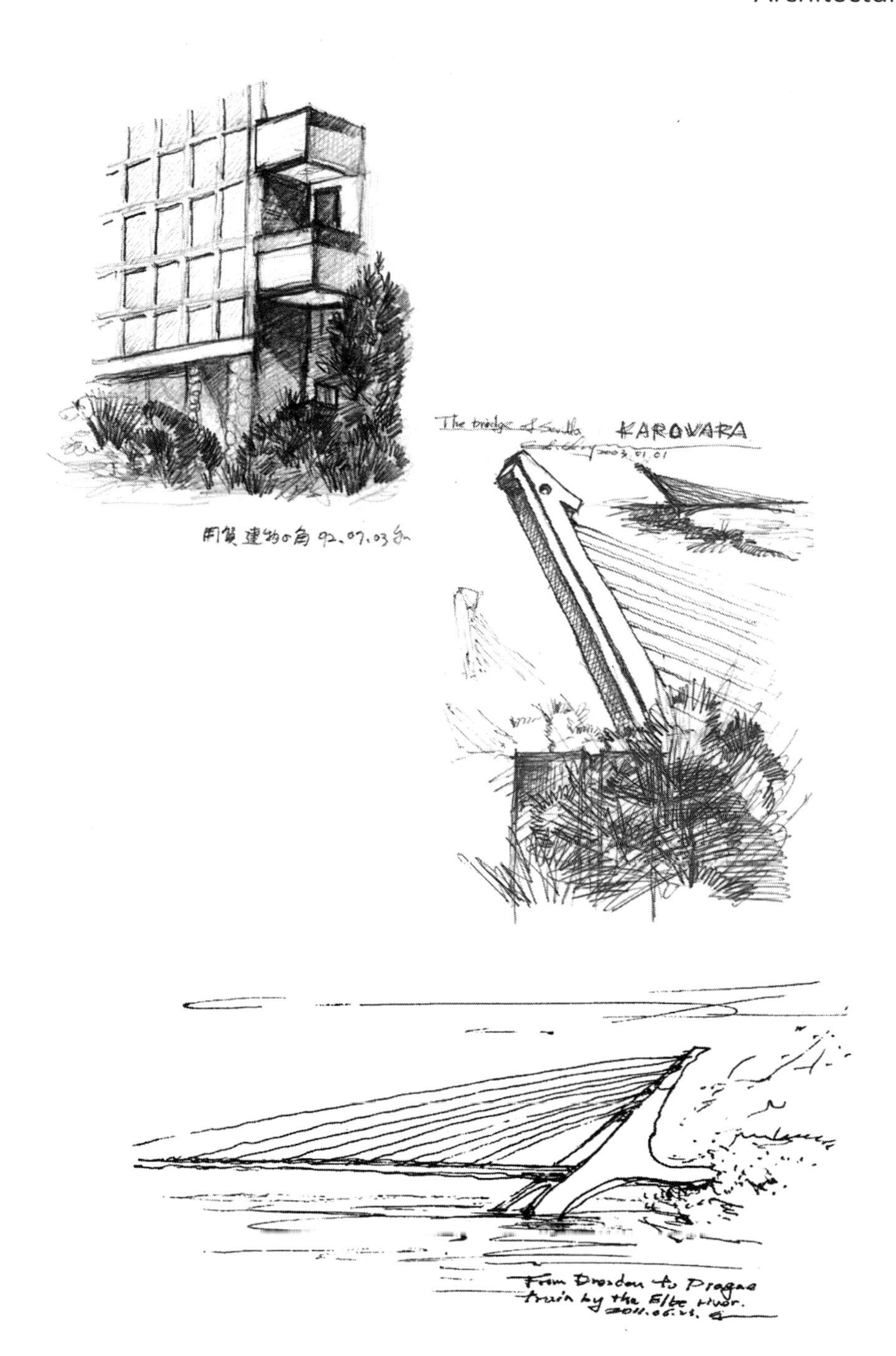
用賀 建物の角 92.07.03
KAROVARA
From Dresdon to Pragae
trein by the Elbe river.
2011.06.21.

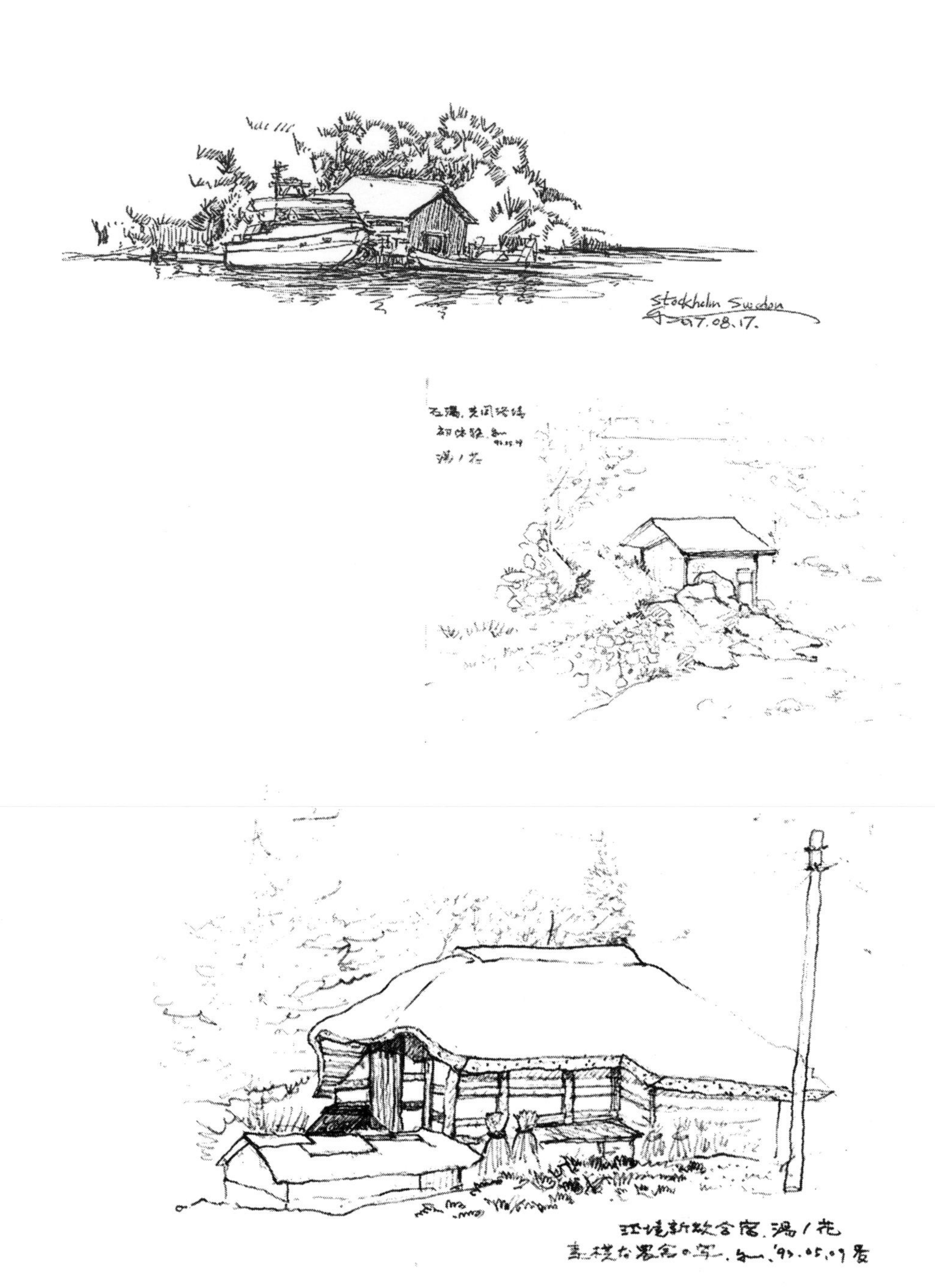
Stockholm Sweden

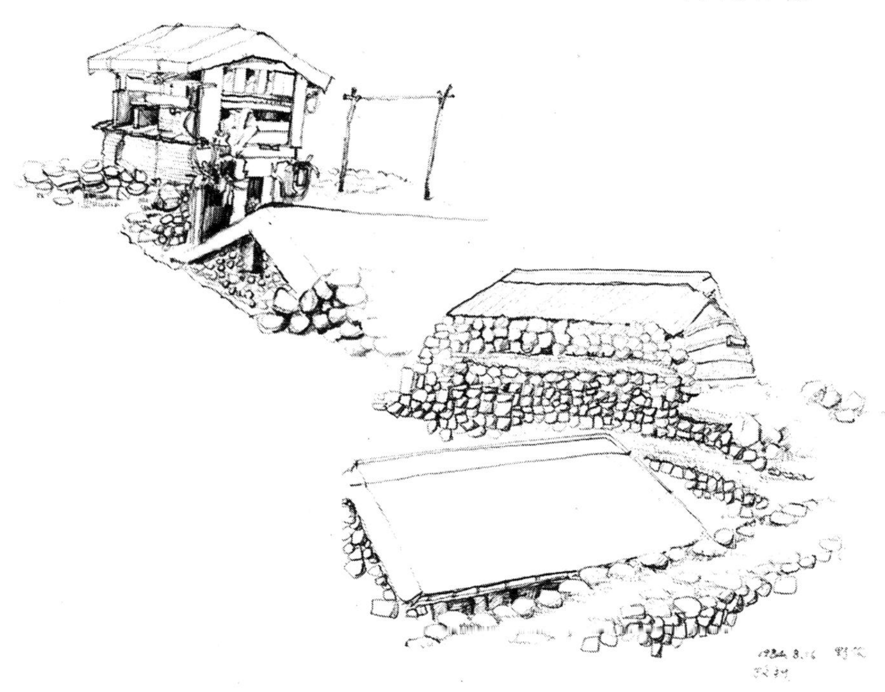

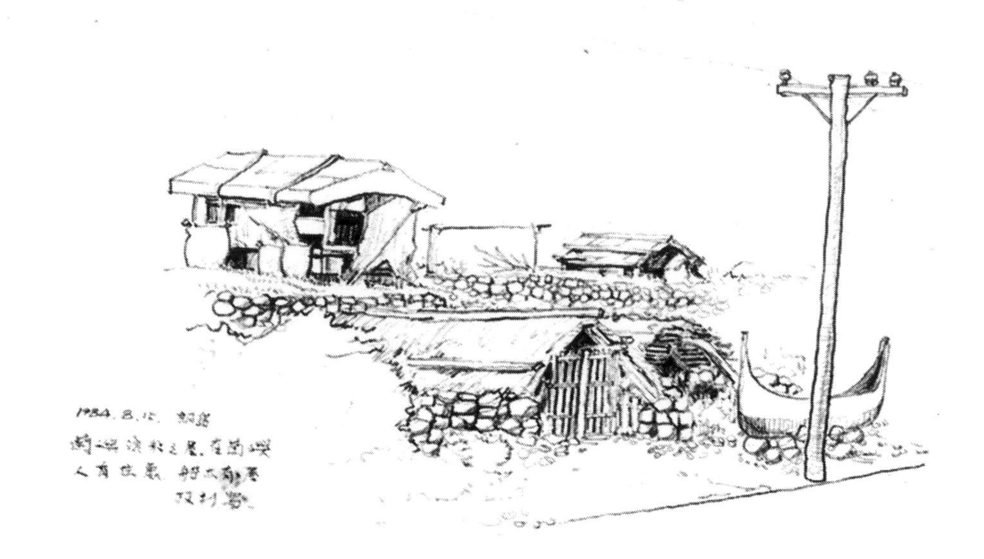
1984.8.12.

1984.8.23

風景

Landscape

風景常常是旅行主要的動機，日常生活中熟悉的景物，往往會讓我們忽視了周遭的美好與感動，旅行中的風景最能直接喚醒這些逐漸遲鈍化的感官……

Landscape scenery is often the main motivation for travel. The familiar scenery in daily life often makes us ignore the beauty and moving around. The landscape scenery during travel can most directly awaken these gradually dulling senses...

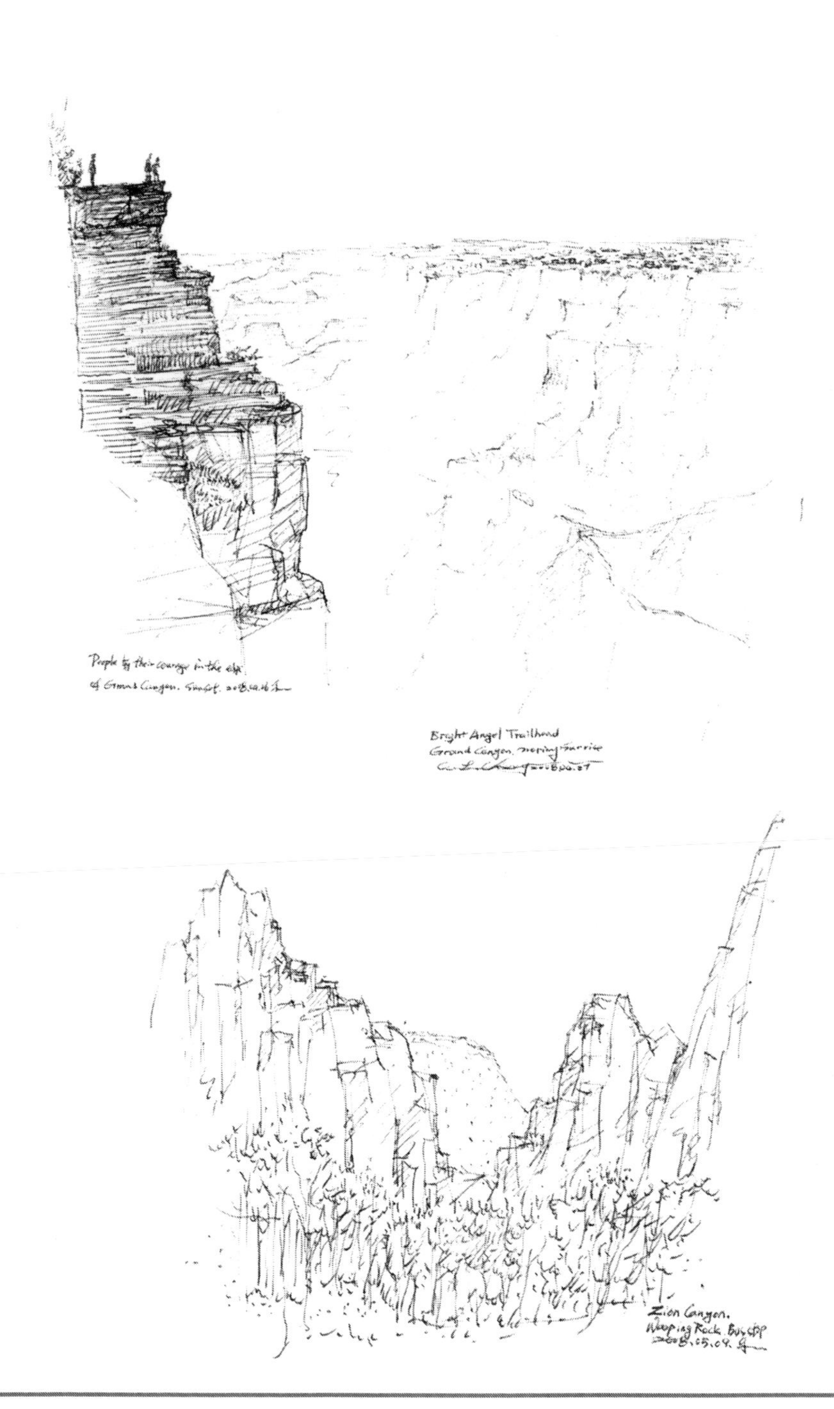
Bright Angel Trailhead
Zion Canyon.
Weeping Rock Bus stop
2008.05.04.

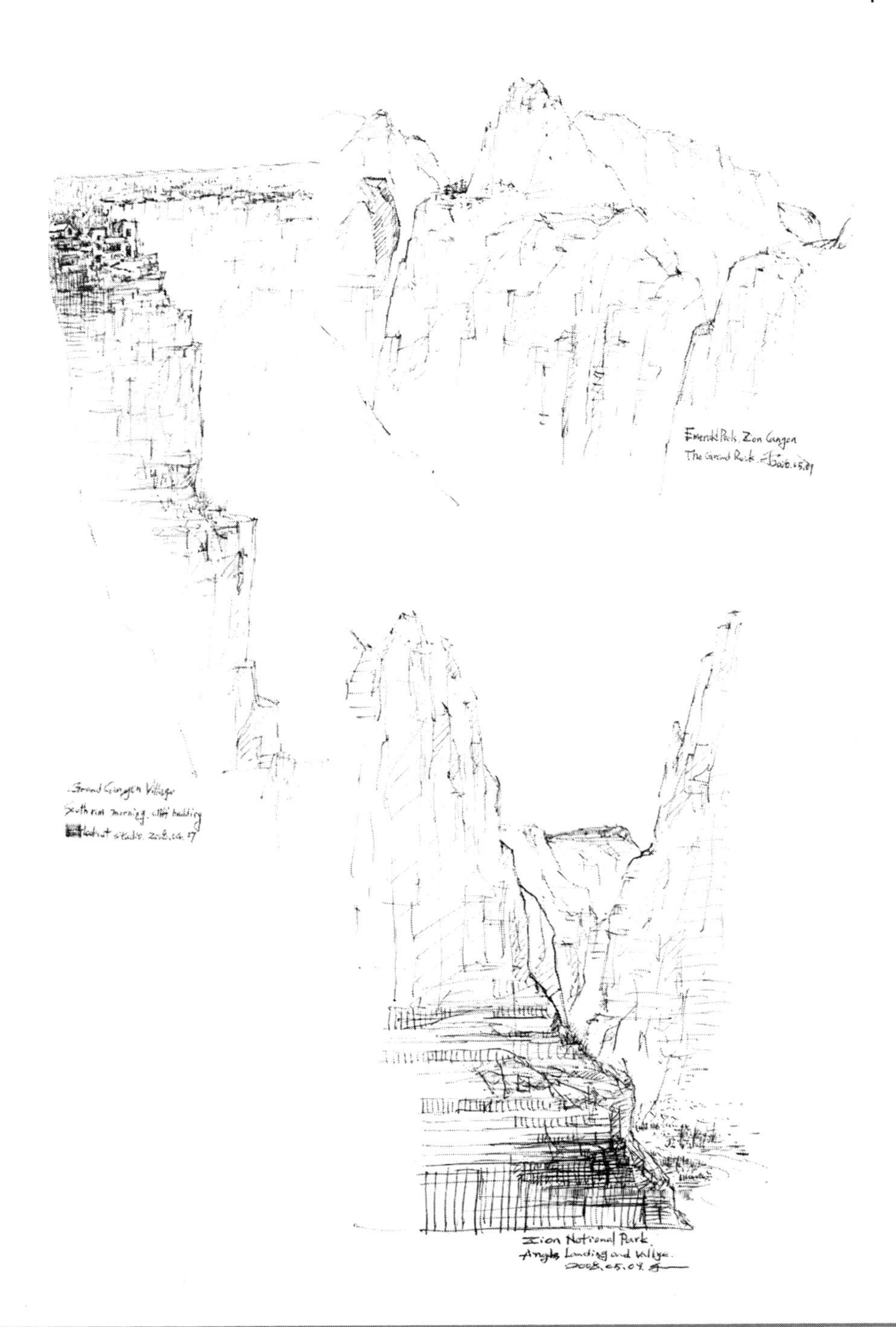
Grand Canyon Village
Zion National Park

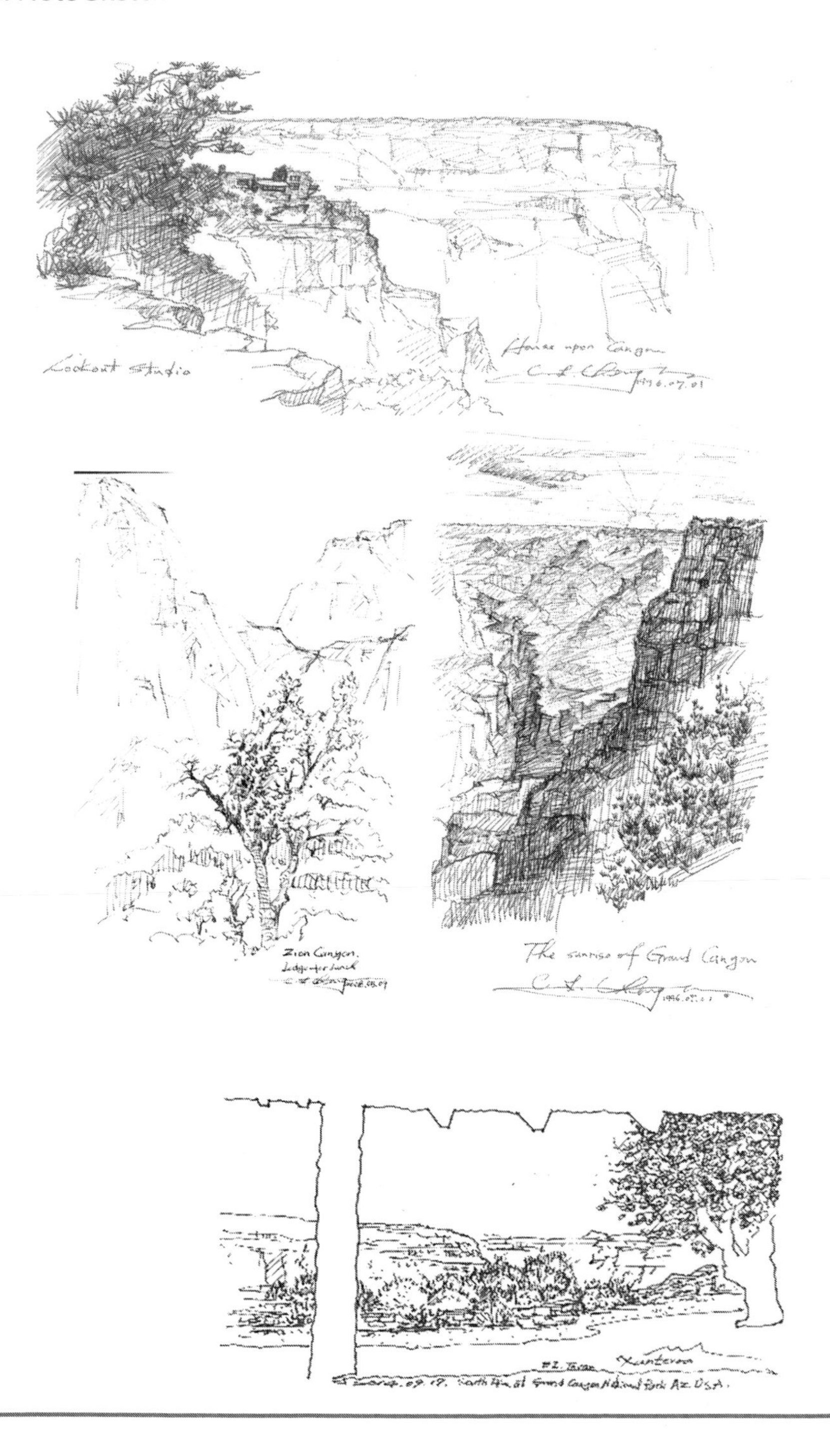
Lookout Studio
House upon Canyon
Zion Canyon
The sunrise of Grand Canyon

Monument Valley 2008.04.26
Dramatic Monument
2008.04.26
A special rock unnamed by the way from Canyon de Chelly to
Mesa Verde. Today I saw it again by the way from Chaco Valley
to Kayenta. So unique and mystery appear upon the horizontal
line as a peaceful guide for a traveler.
2008.04.25

Amazing Valley
Canyon de Chelly. AZ.
Monument Valley, a SCENIC
area. in the world.
Navajo Valley in Canyon de Chelly.
The amizing ruin dwelling.

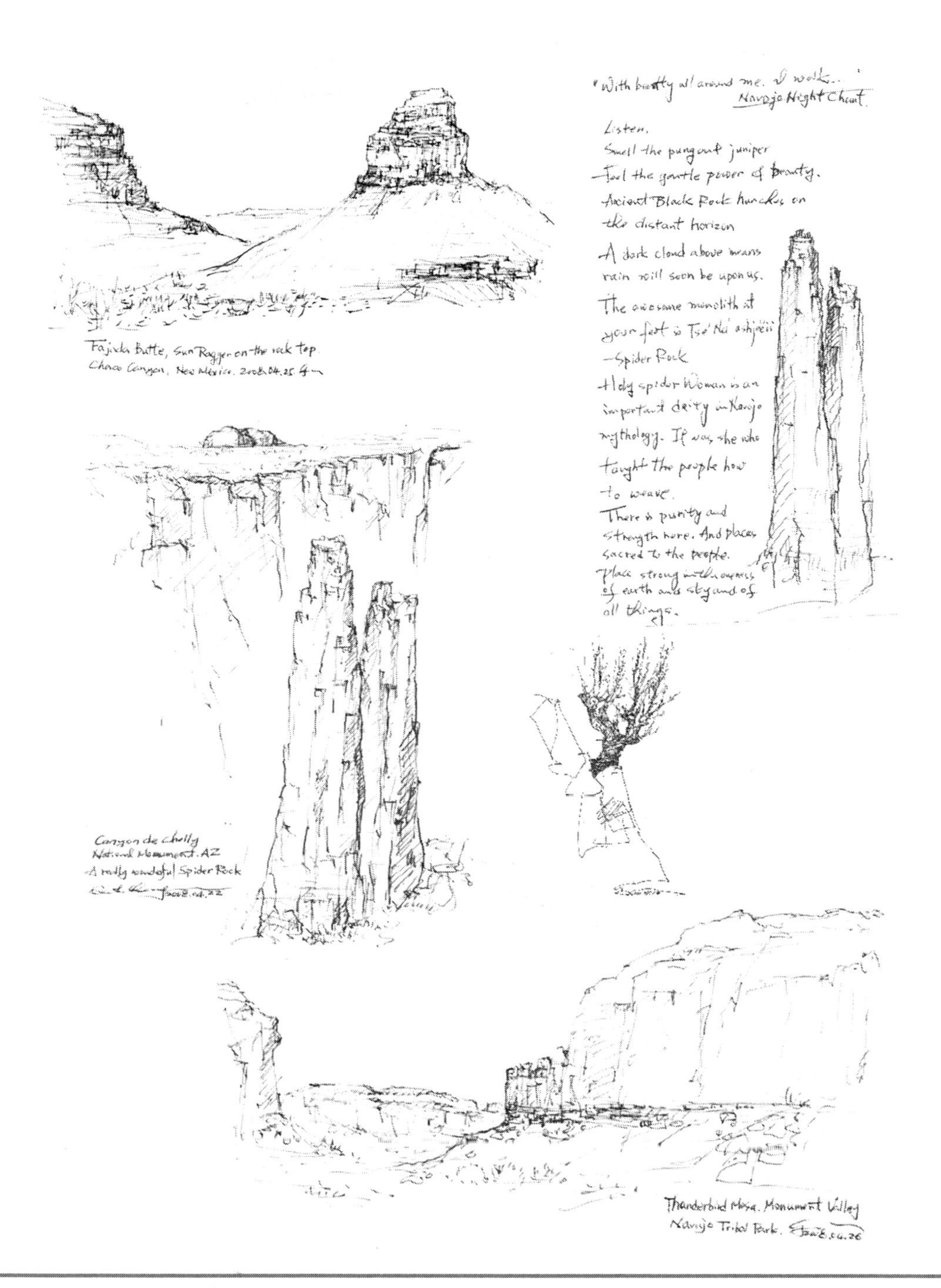
"With beauty all around me. I walk..."
Navajo Night Chant
Listen.
Smell the pungent juniper
Feel the gentle power of beauty.
Ancient Black Rock hunches on
the distant horizon
A dark cloud above means
rain will soon be upon us.
The awesome monolith at
your feet is Tsé Na'ashjéii
—Spider Rock
Holy spider Woman is an
important deity in Navajo
mythology. It was she who
taught the people how
to weave.
There is purity and
strength here. And places
sacred to the people.
Place strong with oneness
of earth and sky and of
all things.
Fajada Butte, Sun Dagger on the rock top
Chaco Canyon, New Mexico. 2008.04.25.
Canyon de Chelly
National Monument. AZ
A really wonderful Spider Rock
2008.04.22
Thunderbird Mesa. Monument Valley
Navajo Tribal Park. 2008.04.26

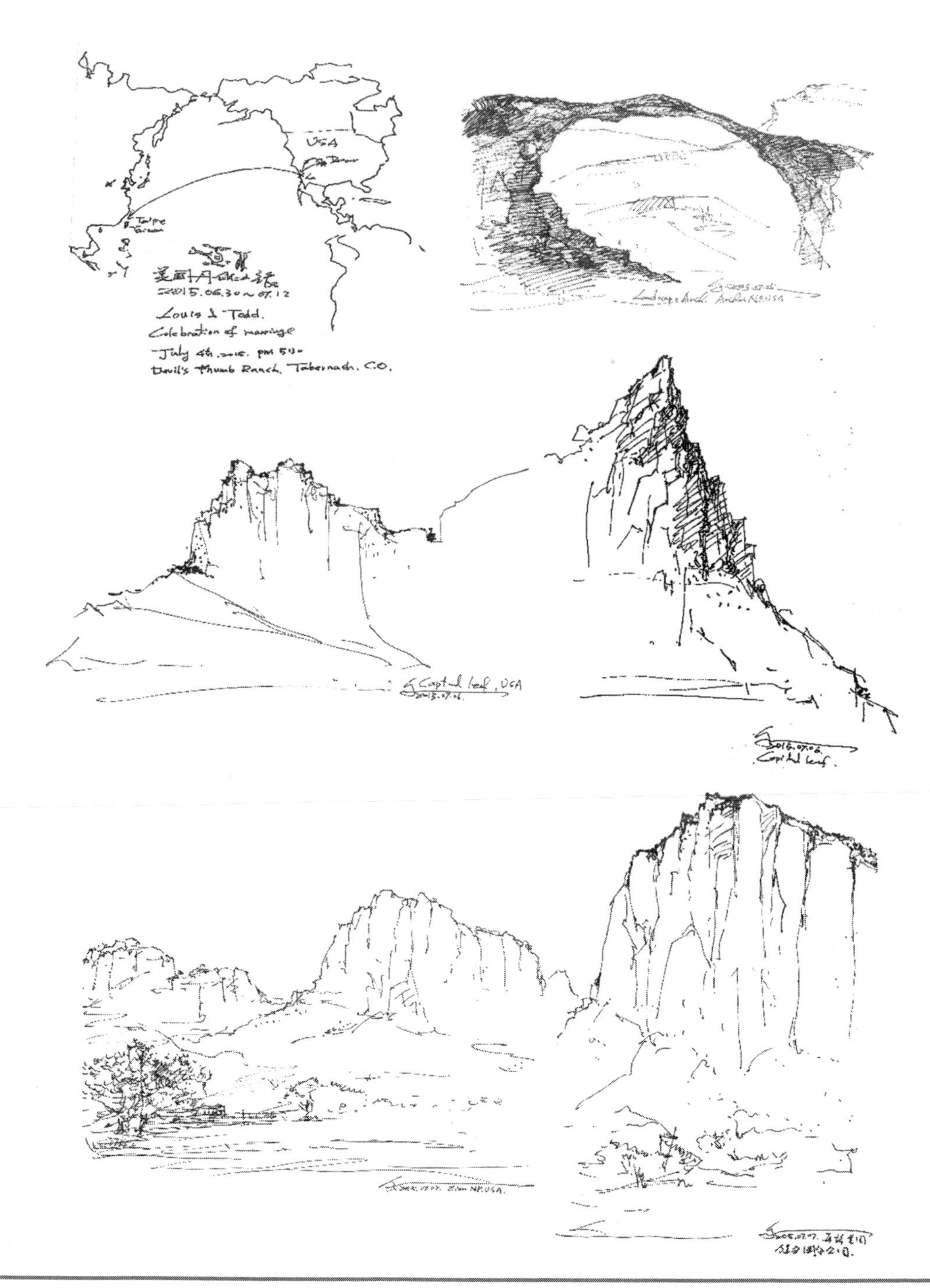
USA
Louis & Todd.
Celebration of marriage

2015. Zion NP. USA
2015.07.08
Grand Canyon
Lipanpoint. USA
A wonderful sunset with
brother, sister and Andy
2015.07.07. Zion USA
2015.07.07 Zion
NP USA.

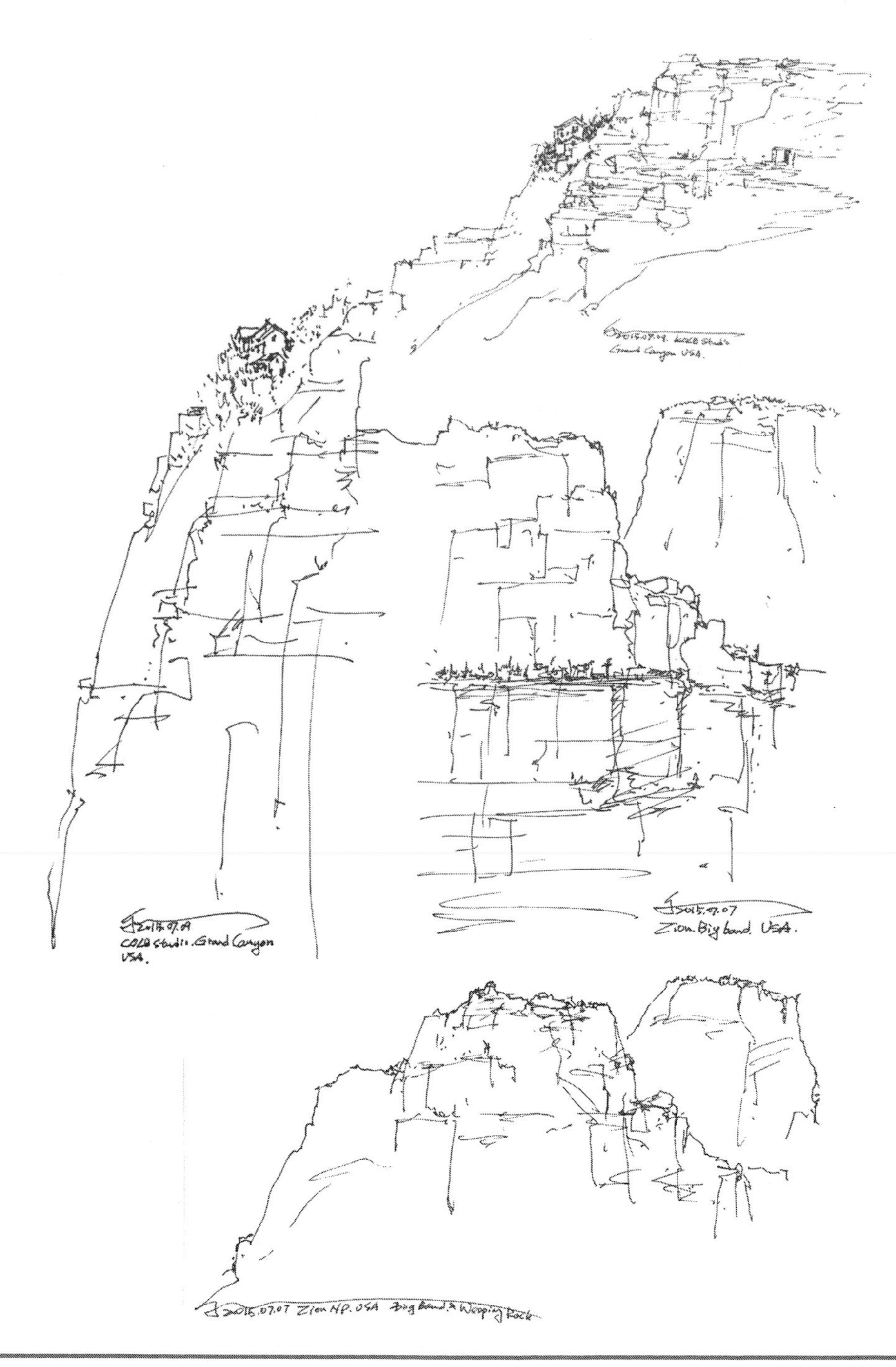
Grand Canyon USA.
2015.07.09
Grand Canyon
USA.
2015.07.07
Zion. Big band. USA.
2015.07.07 Zion NP. USA Big Band & Weeping Rock

The Lookout
KOLB STUDIO

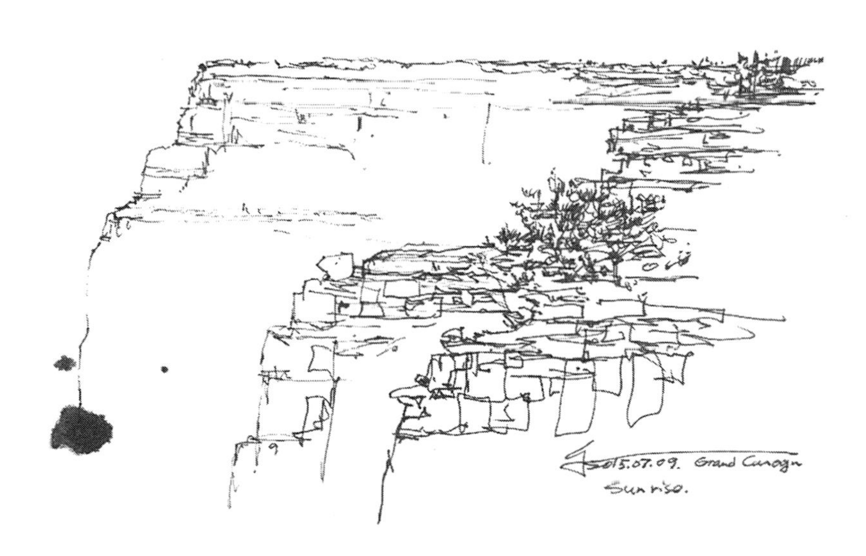

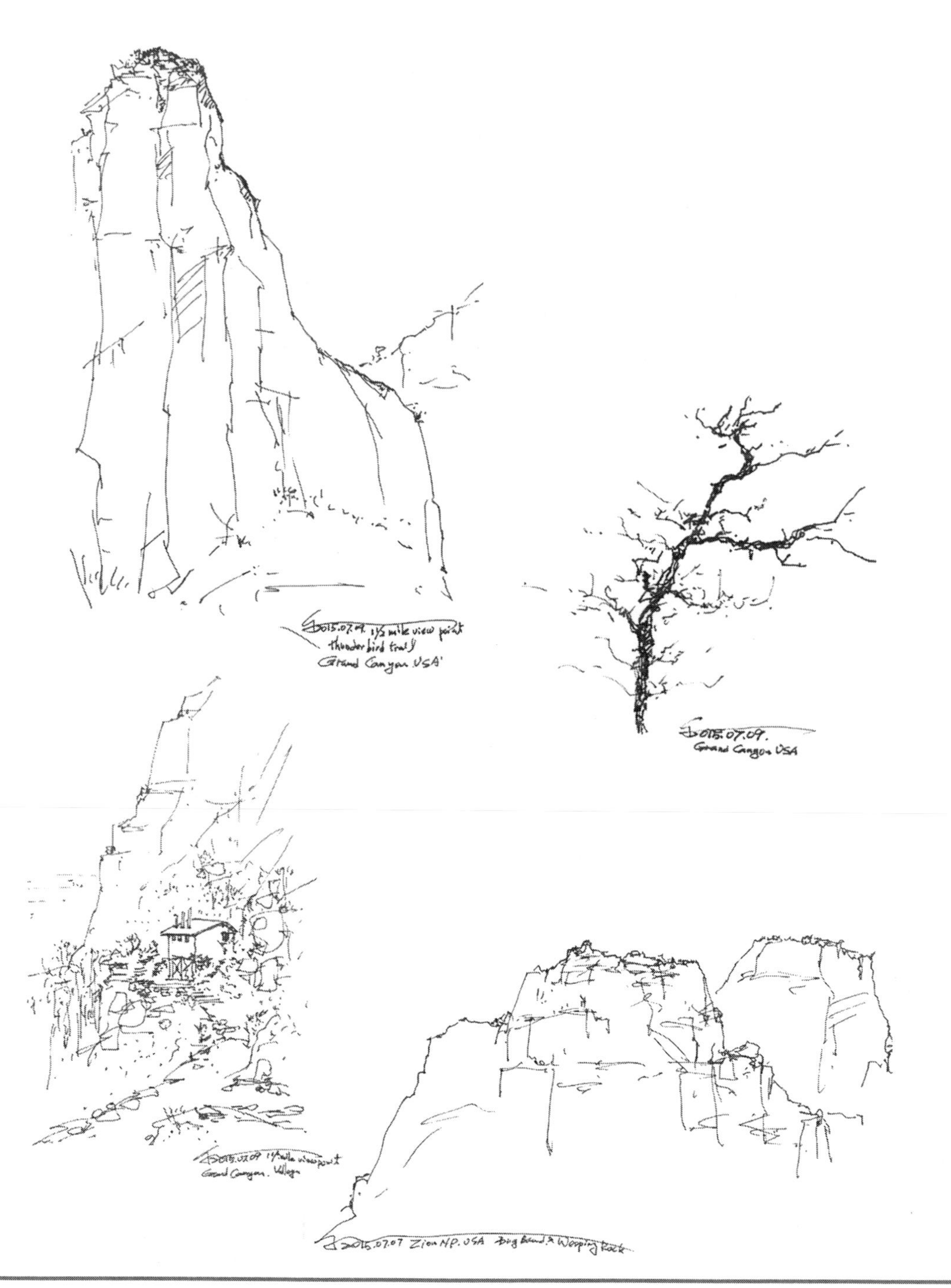
2015.07.09 1/2 mile view point
thunder bird trail
Grand Canyon USA
2015.07.09.
Grand Canyon USA
2015.07.09 1/2 mile viewpoint
Grand Canyon. Village
2015.07.07 Zion NP. USA Big Bend & Weeping Rock

Lake Tahoe, masterpiece of Nature
Carson city visiting. 2008.05.03

The early morning of Salt Lake is so quiet.
and so beautifully. on the way to Yellowstone.
Salt Lake City 2008.05.05

Big Bear Lake. A peaceful morning
2008.05.10

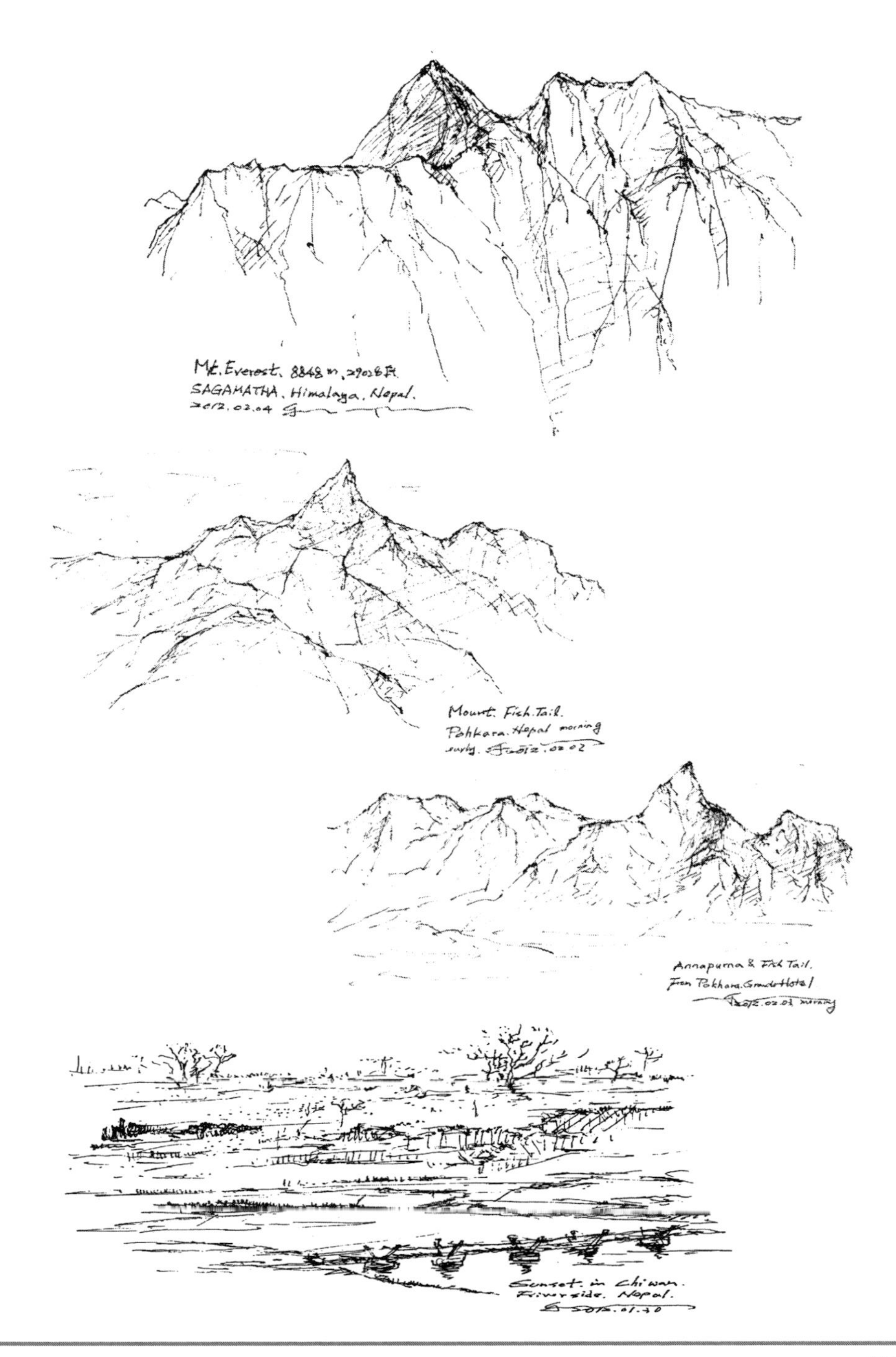
Mt. Everest. 8848 m, 29028 ft.
SAGAMATHA. Himalaya. Nepal.
Mount. Fish. Tail.
Pohkara. Nepal morning
Annapurna & Fish Tail.
From Pokhara. Grande Hotel
Sunset. in Chiwan.
Riverside. Nepal.

Chitwan National Park
Nepal 2012.01.30
Fish Tail. Pohkara.
Nepal 2012.02.02
Fewa Wildlife Resort. Chitwan National Park
Nepal. 2012.01.30
Boating in Phewa Lake
A Place lik Sun moon Lake
Pohkara. Nepal.
2012.02.02

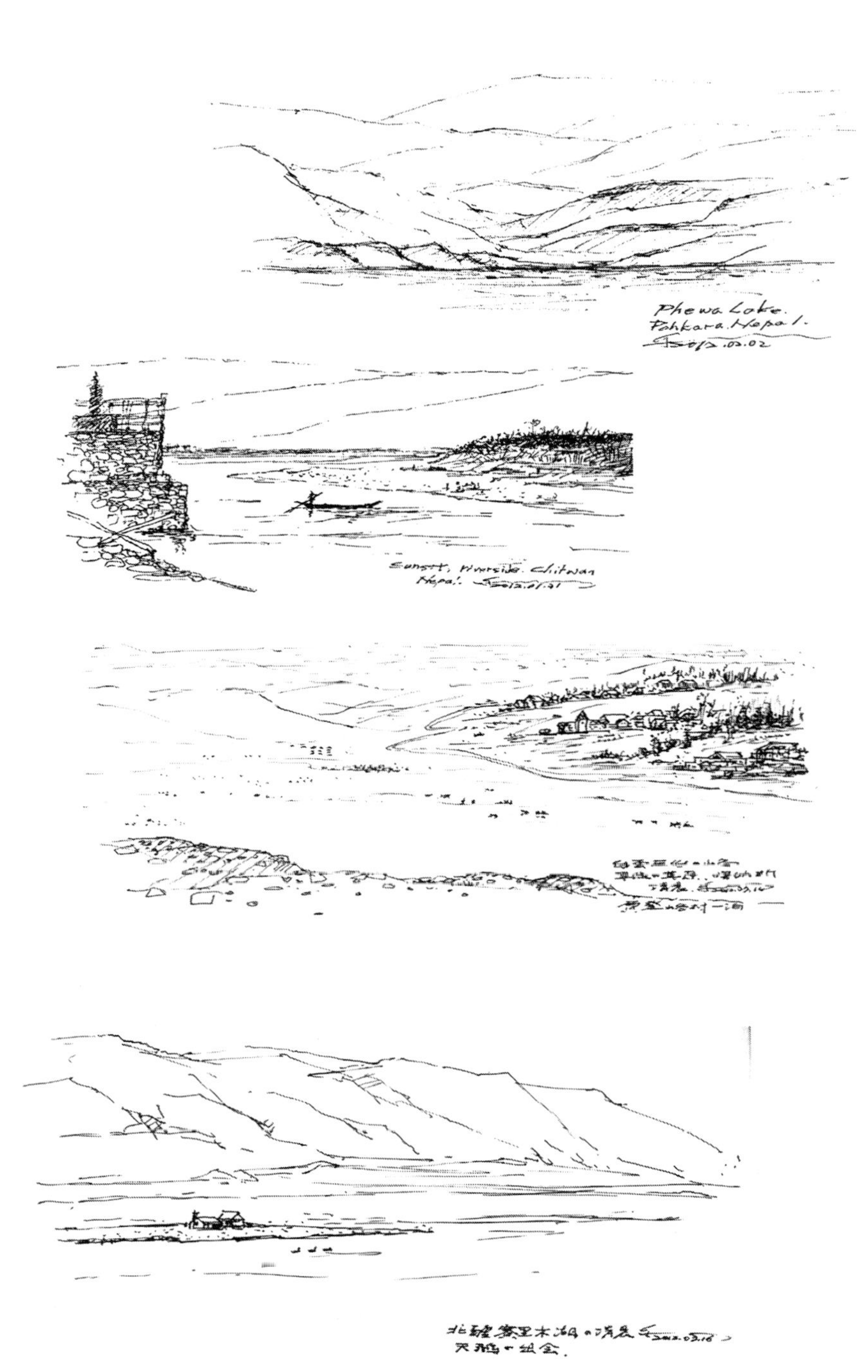
Phewa Lake.
Pohkara. Nepal.
Sunset, Riverside. Chitwan
Nepal.

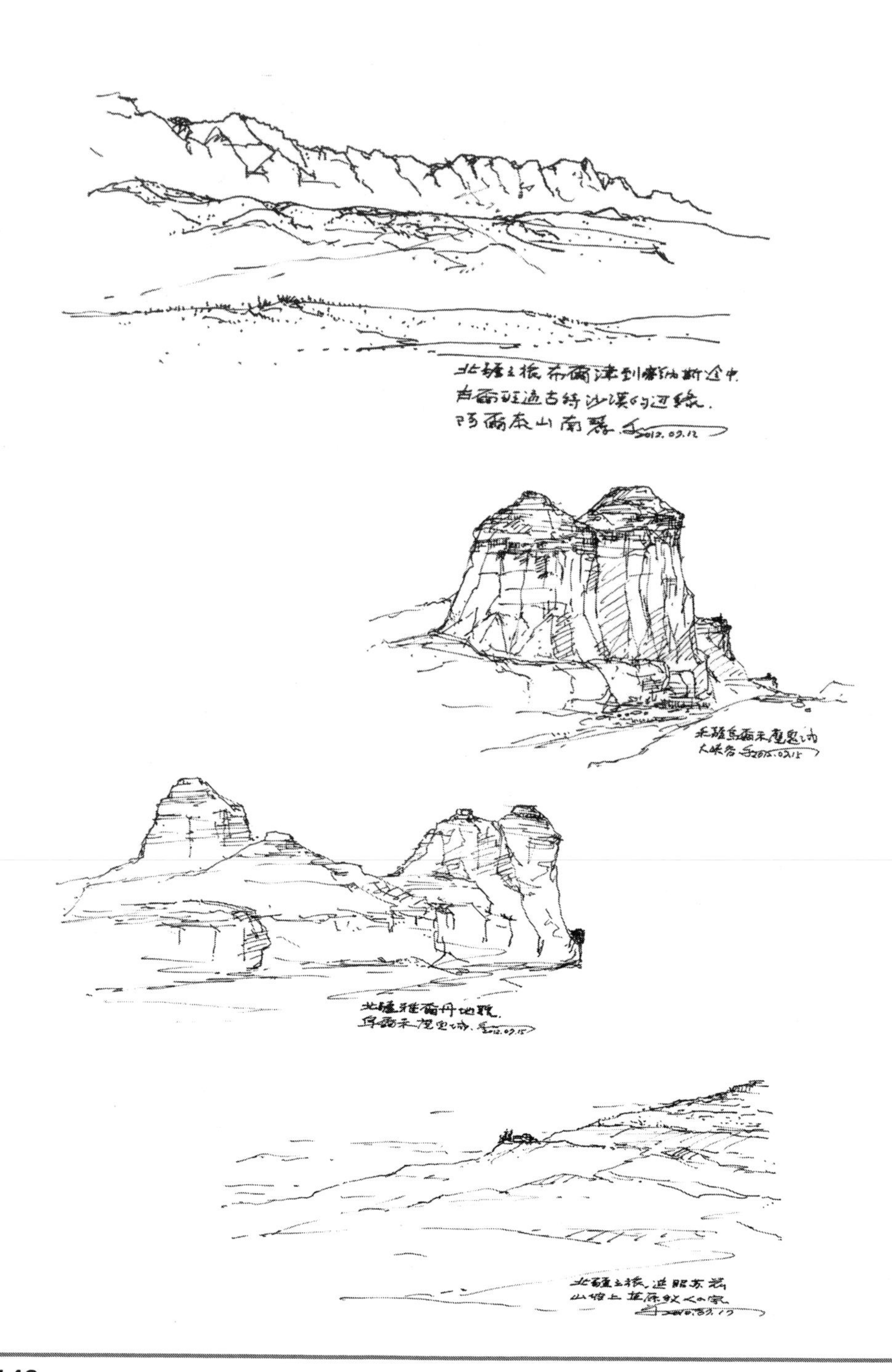
北疆之旅 布爾津到哈納斯途中
古爾班通古特沙漠的邊緣
阿爾泰山南麓 2012.07.12
北疆烏爾禾魔鬼城
大峽谷 2012.07.15
北疆雅丹地貌
烏爾禾魔鬼城 2012.07.15
北疆之旅 進昭蘇
山坡上 哈薩克人の家
2012.07.17

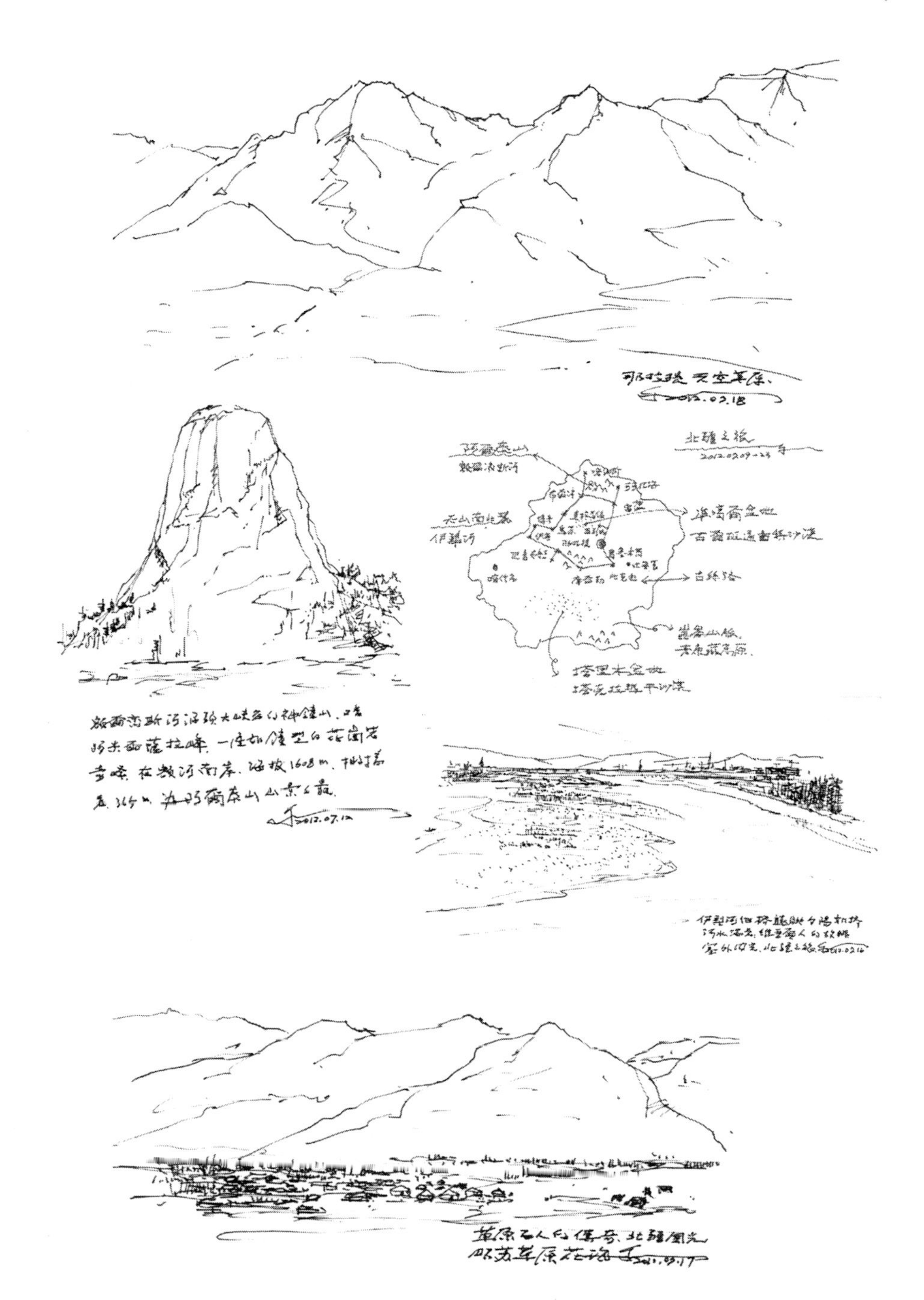
那拉提 空中草原
2012.07.18
北疆之旅
2012.02.09-23
阿爾泰山
額爾齊斯河
天山南北麓
伊犁河
準噶爾盆地
古爾班通古特沙漠
崑崙山脈
塔里木盆地
塔克拉瑪干沙漠
額爾齊斯河河頭大峽谷的神鐘山，中名
阿米爾薩拉峰，一座如鐘型的花崗岩
奇峰，在該河南岸，海拔1608m，相對高
差365m，為阿爾泰山山景之最。
2012.07.12
草原石人的傳奇，北疆風光
昭蘇草原花海
2012.07.17

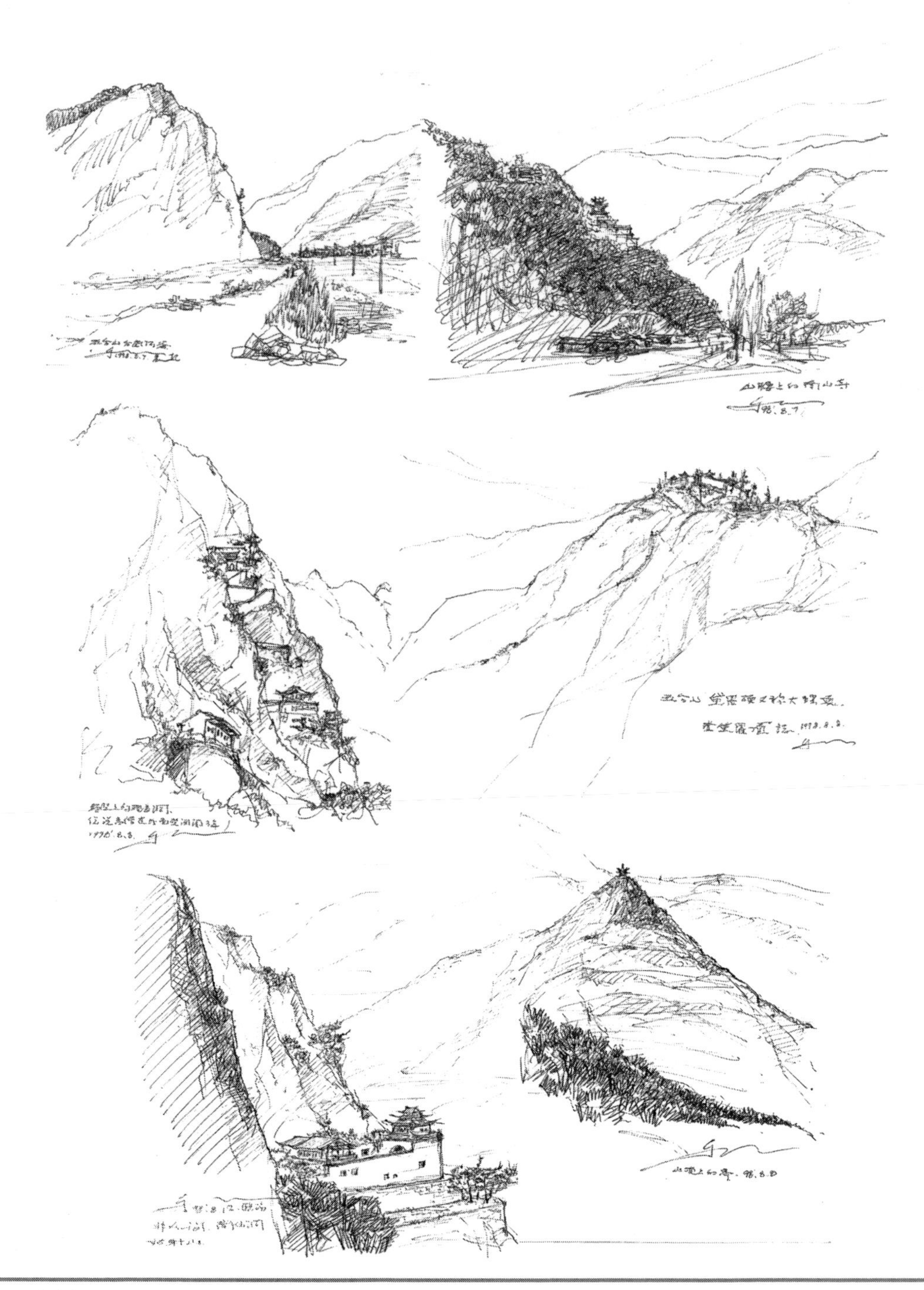

新疆托克遜縣境內甘溝路段
北疆額爾齊斯河畔
五彩灘.雅丹地形
2012.07.14
新疆那拉提大草原
騎馬道旁的風光
2012.07.18

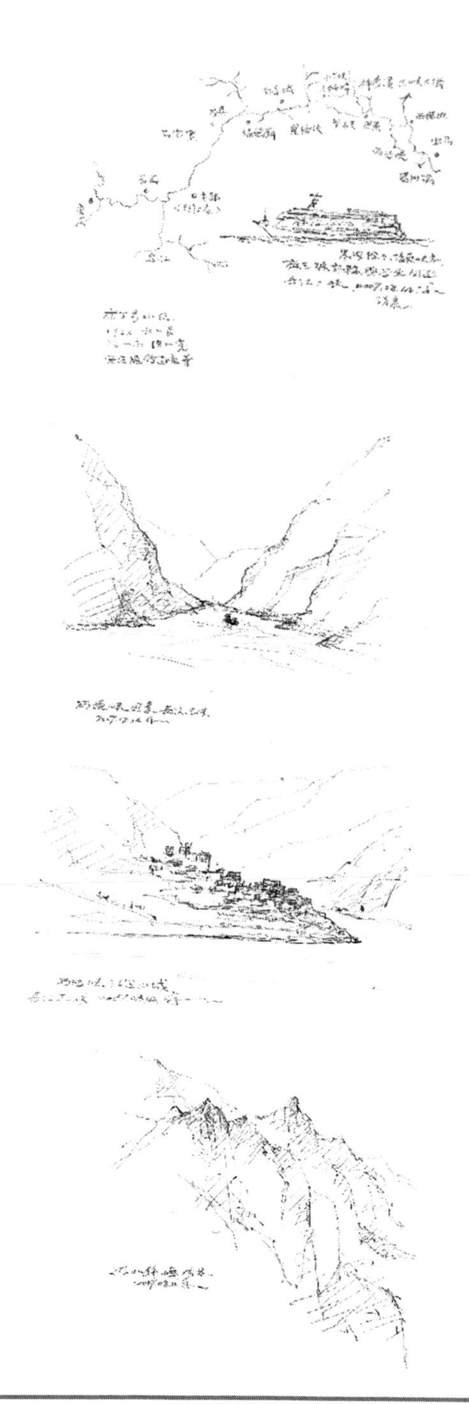

天穹蒼蒼鴻雁飛
峽猶重重江水流
帝王頂上晨曦清
師生同遊三峽景

宜昌的清晨，三峽的起點。
合科大師生15人，我、生、家王
弓郭輔，同遊三峽奇景。
清晨站在上甲板，打完太極
清爽快意，仿古人藏詩一首
以為回憶。2007.08.14. 丞

天邊月芽彎如鈎
江心風清搖輕舟
帝王郵輪曉席散
遊遍三峽仍意猶

2007.08.16.

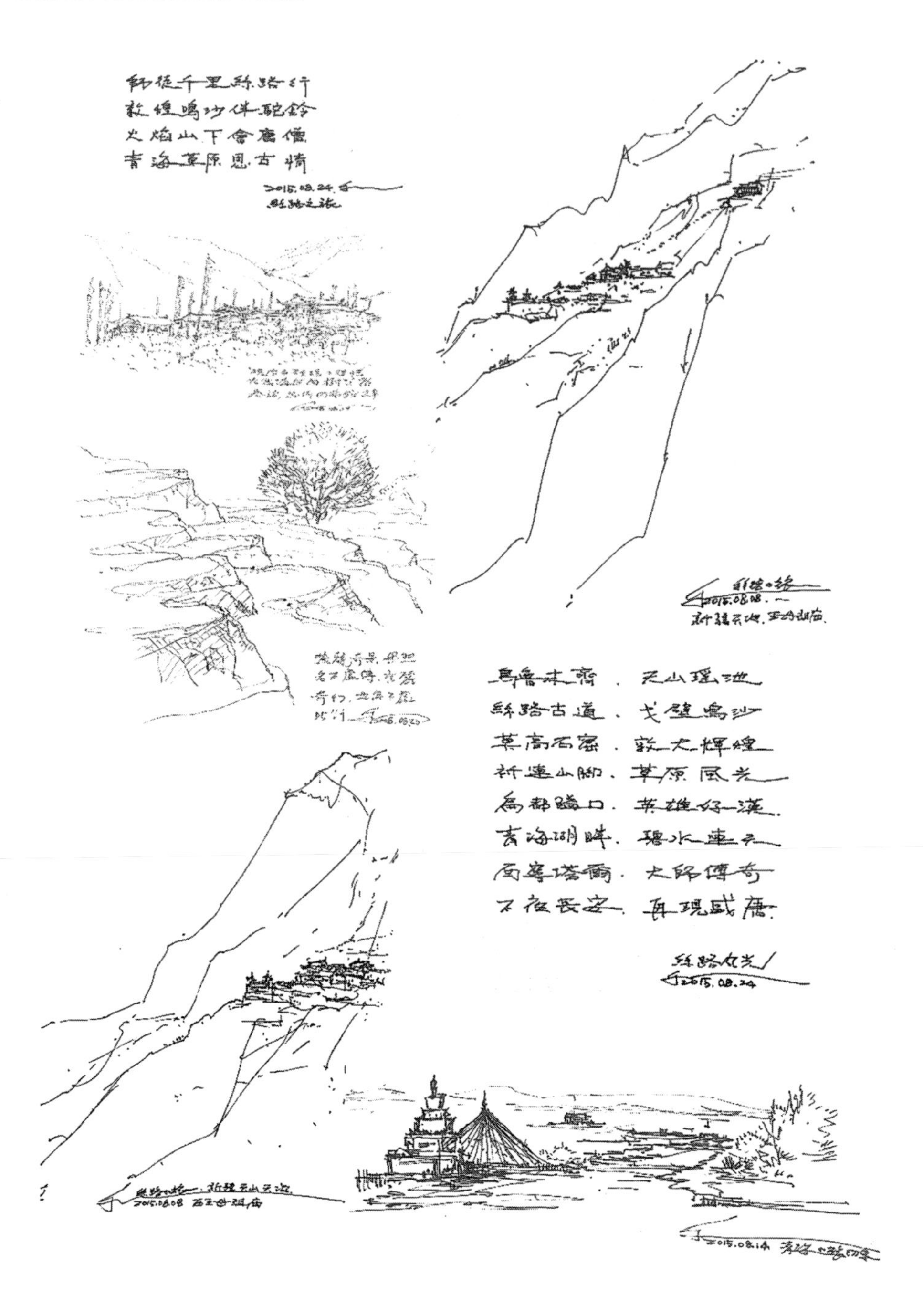
敦煌鳴沙伴駝鈴
火焰山下會唐僧
青海草原思古情
2015.08.24
烏魯木齊．天山瑤池
絲路古道．戈壁鳴沙
莫高石窟．敦大輝煌
祁連山腳．草原風光
英雄好漢
青海湖畔．碧水連天
西寧塔爾．大師傳奇
不在長安．再現盛唐
絲路風光
2015.08.24

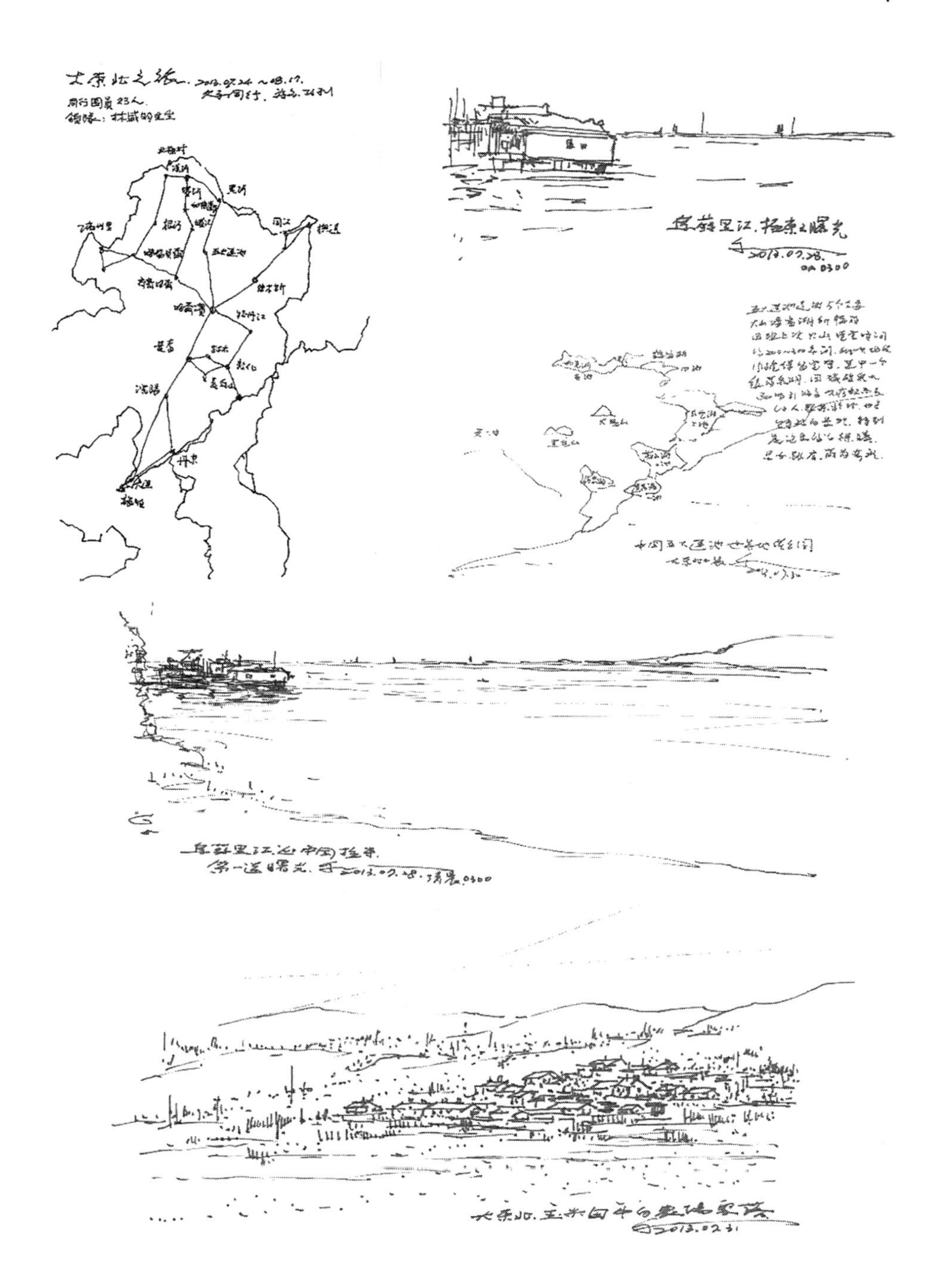
大東北之旅 2013.07.24～08.17.
同行團員23人.
烏蘇里江.極東之曙光
2013.07.28.
AM 0300
烏蘇里江沿中國極東.
第一道曙光.
2013.07.28.清晨0300

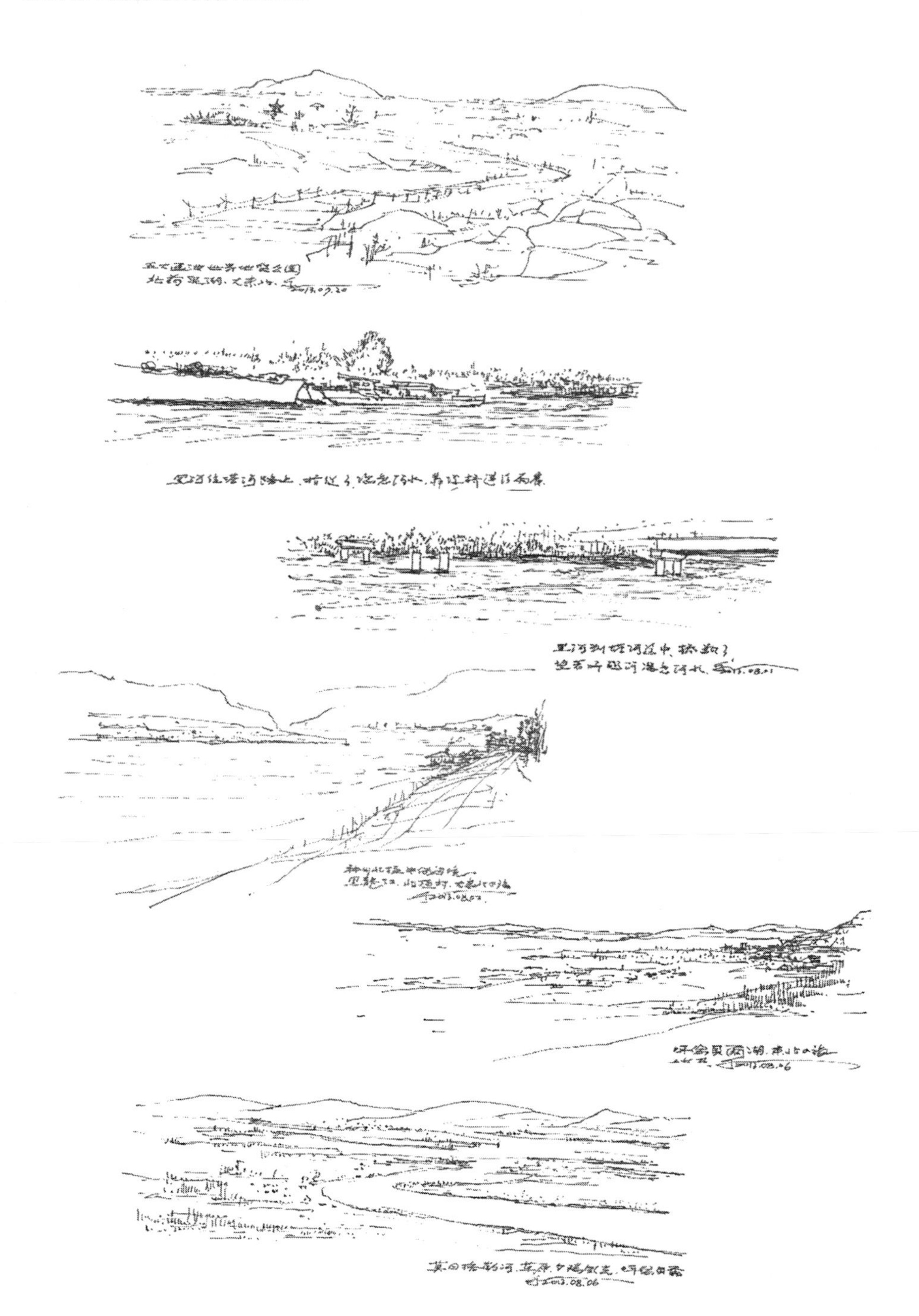

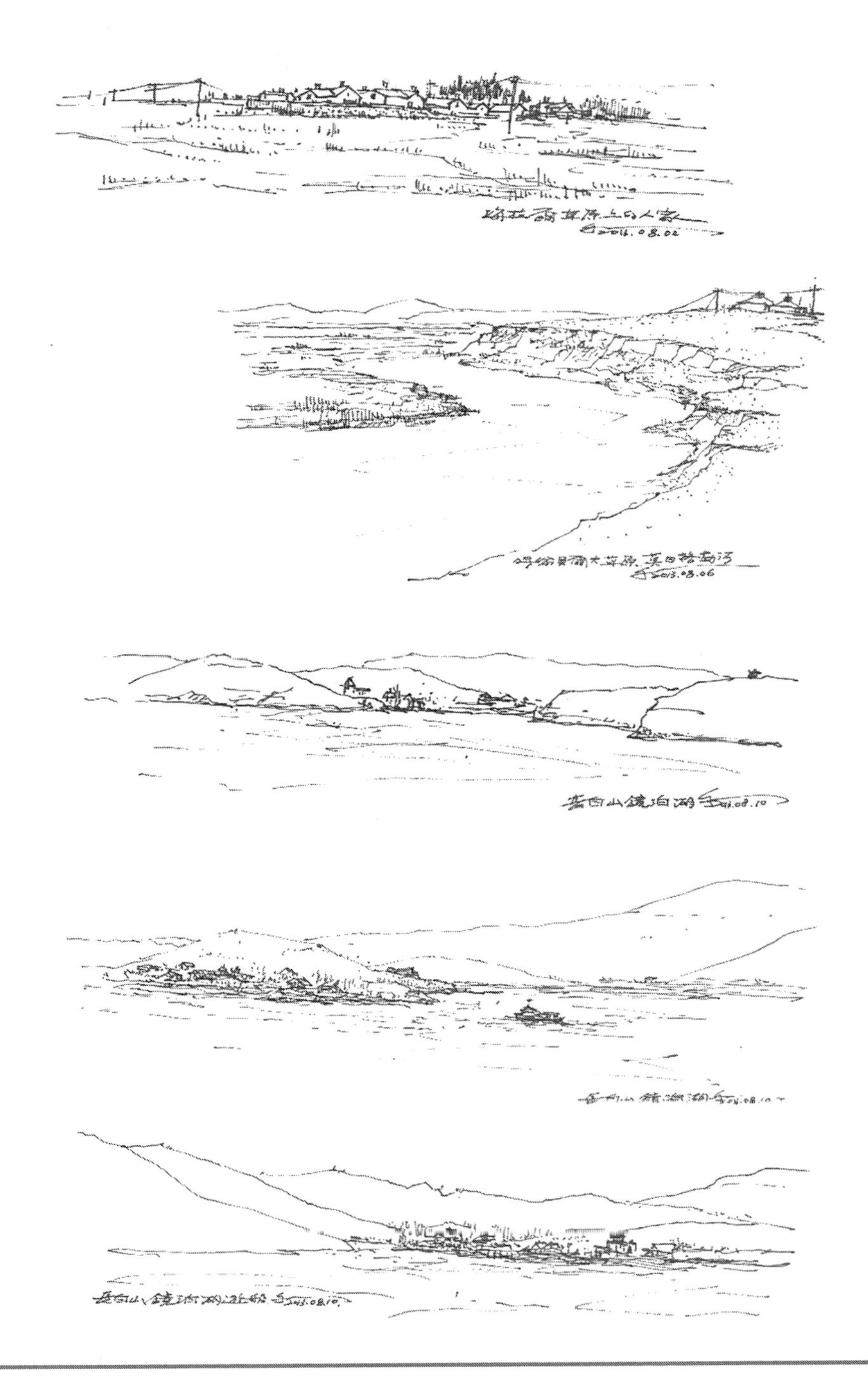

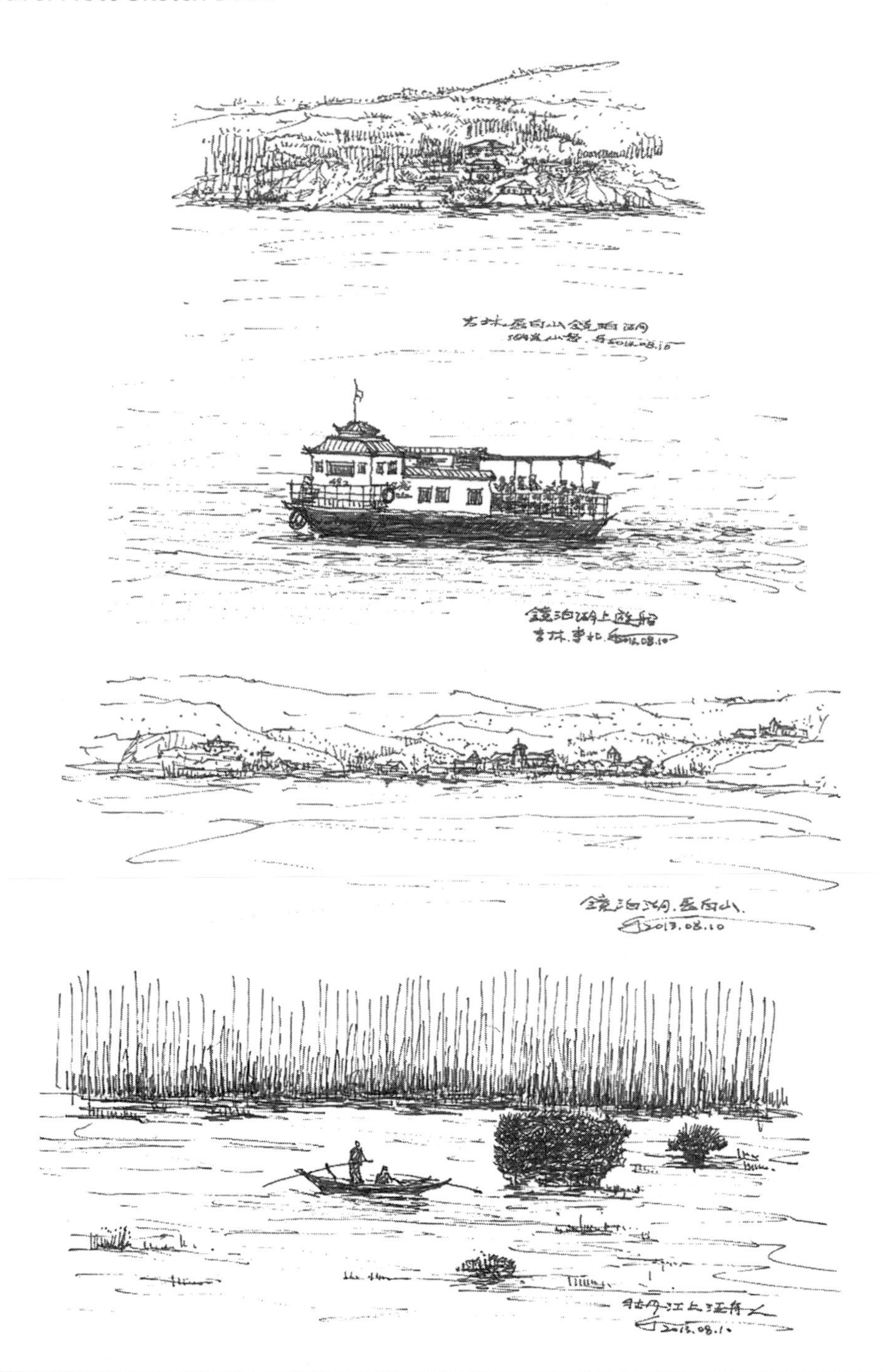
鏡泊湖上遊船
鏡泊湖.
2013.08.10

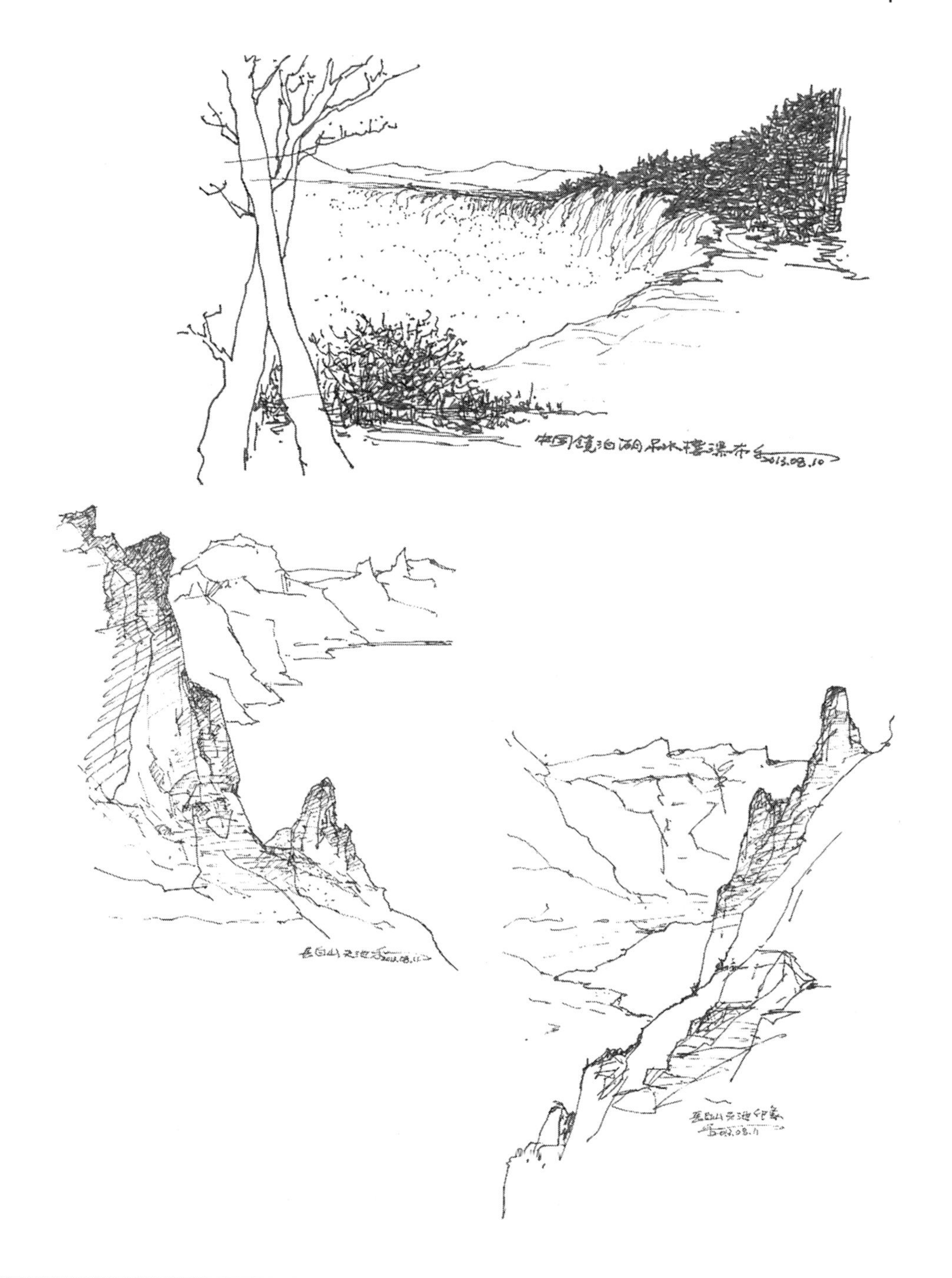
中国鏡泊湖吊水樓瀑布 2013.08.10
長白山天池
長白山天池印象

North. Vietnam. Hà Noi
2013.02.22.
~26.
CHINA
The image of the Long Bay, Vietnam
2013.02.23
A quick picture.
Ha Long Bay. Vietnam
2013.02.23
Ha Long Bay. Vietnam. 2013.02.23

HaLong Bay. Vietnam.
River. HoiAn. VietNam
Saling bowt. over the sea.
HaLong Bay. Vietnam.
The acient town biside the river.
HoiAn. Viet-Nam.

Hotel Cetus, Amalfi Coast.
Capri.
2013.04.17.

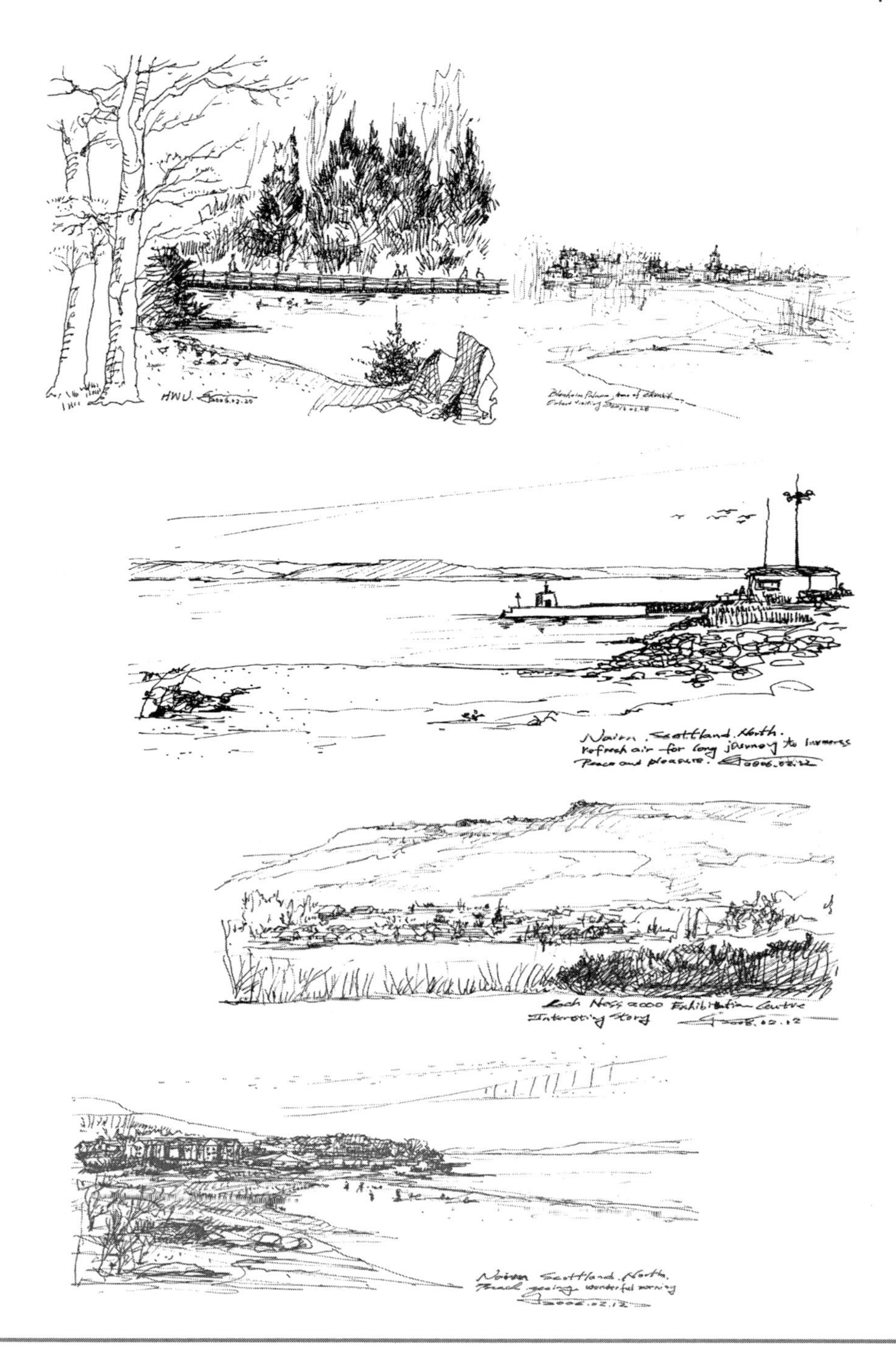
HWU.
Nairn . Scottland . North.
Refresh air - for long journey to Inverness
Peace and pleasure. 2006.02.12
Loch Ness 2000 Exhibition Centre
Interesting Story
Nairn Scottland . North.
Beach going, wonderful morning
2006.02.12

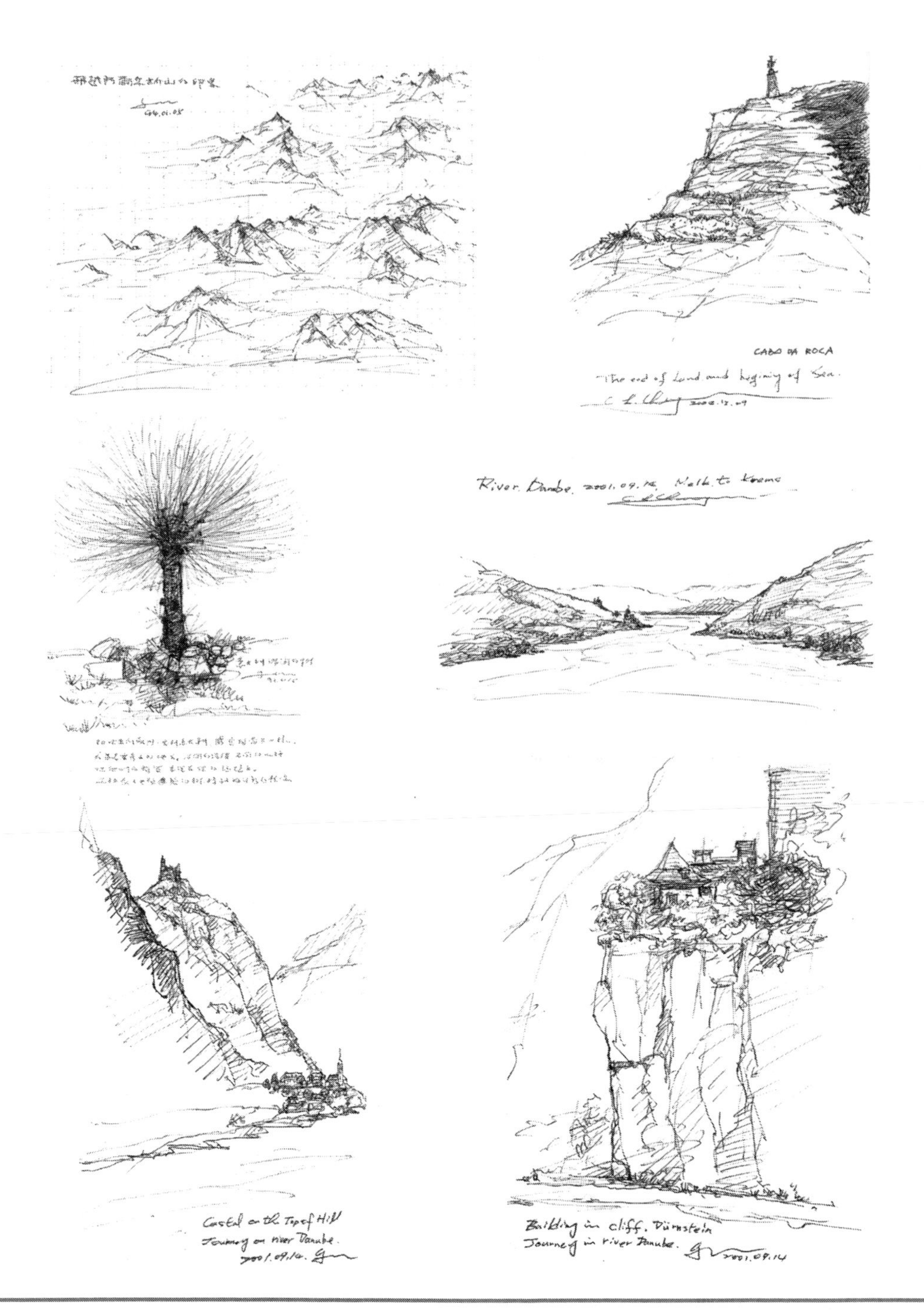
CABO DA ROCA
The end of Land and beginning of Sea.
River Danube. 2001.09.14.
Castel on the Top of Hill
Journey on river Danube.
2001.09.14.
Building in cliff. Dürnstein
Journey in river Danube.
2001.09.14

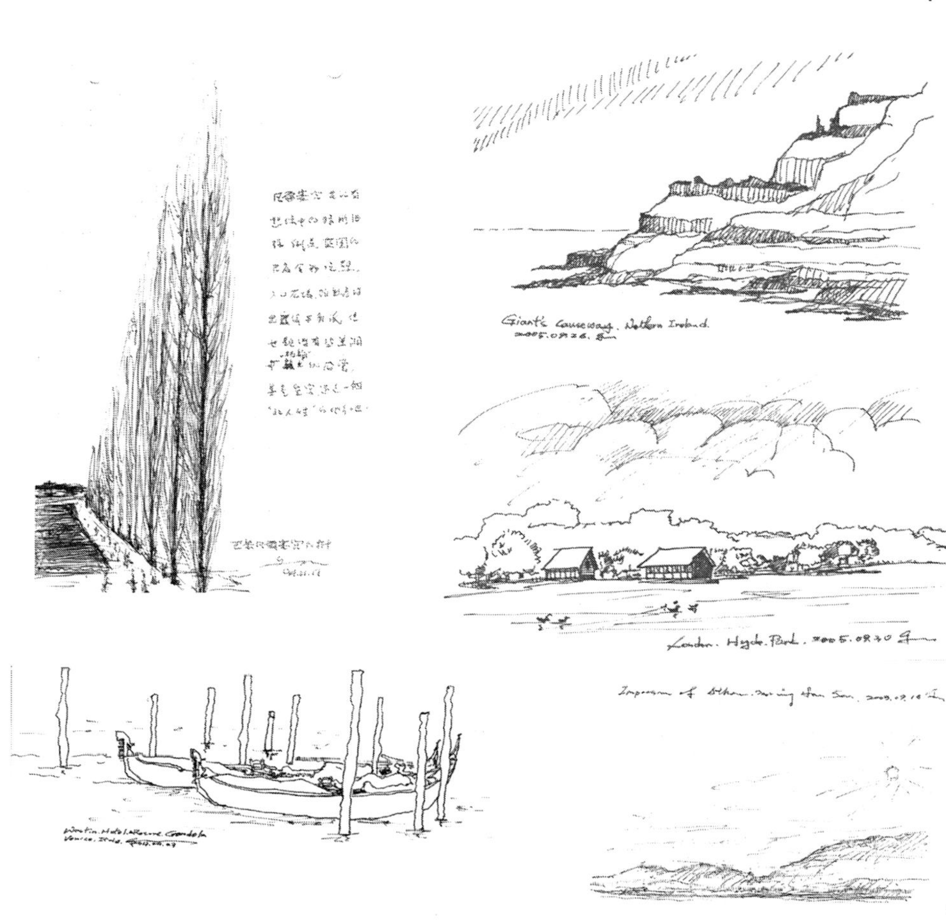
Giant's Causeway. Nothern Ireland.
London. Hyde. Park. 2005.09.30

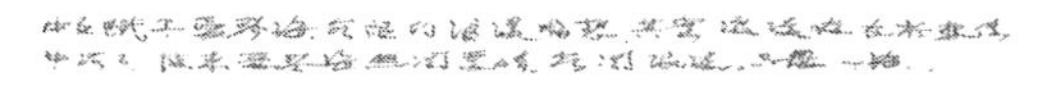

A perfect day for Aegean Sea.

Cannes, France
Provence, France
Chamonix
Mont-BLANC
Courmageur
Auberge de La
Hungary Farm land.
views from train.

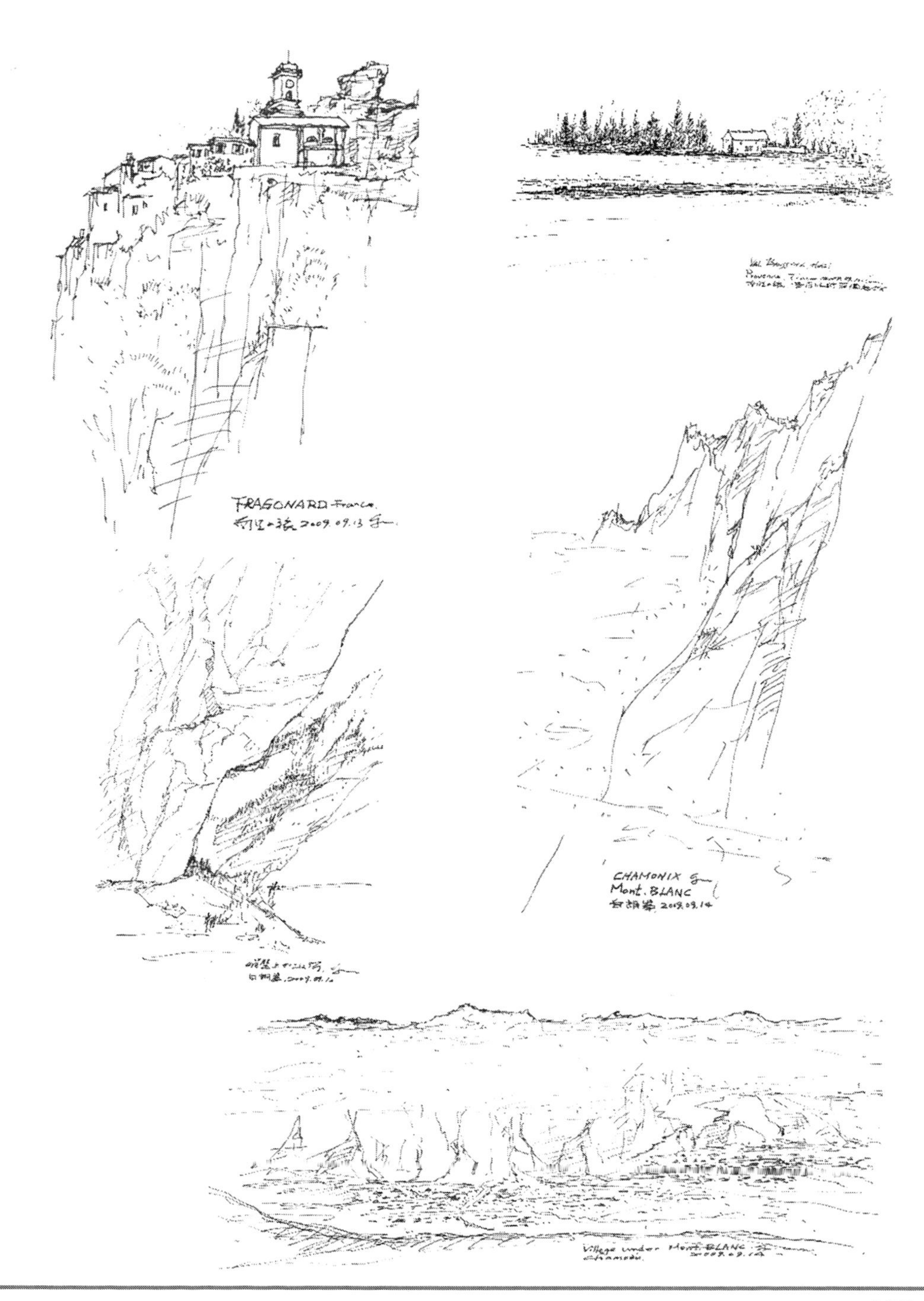
FRAGONARD France
CHAMONIX
Mont. BLANC
Village under Mont BLANC

Ulvik. Brakanes Hotel, Hardanger
Norway 2017.08.12
Stalheim Turist Hotel
Stalheim Norway 2017.08.13
Silja Line 2017.08.17
Amazing Hotel.
STALHEIM, Norway
2017.08.13

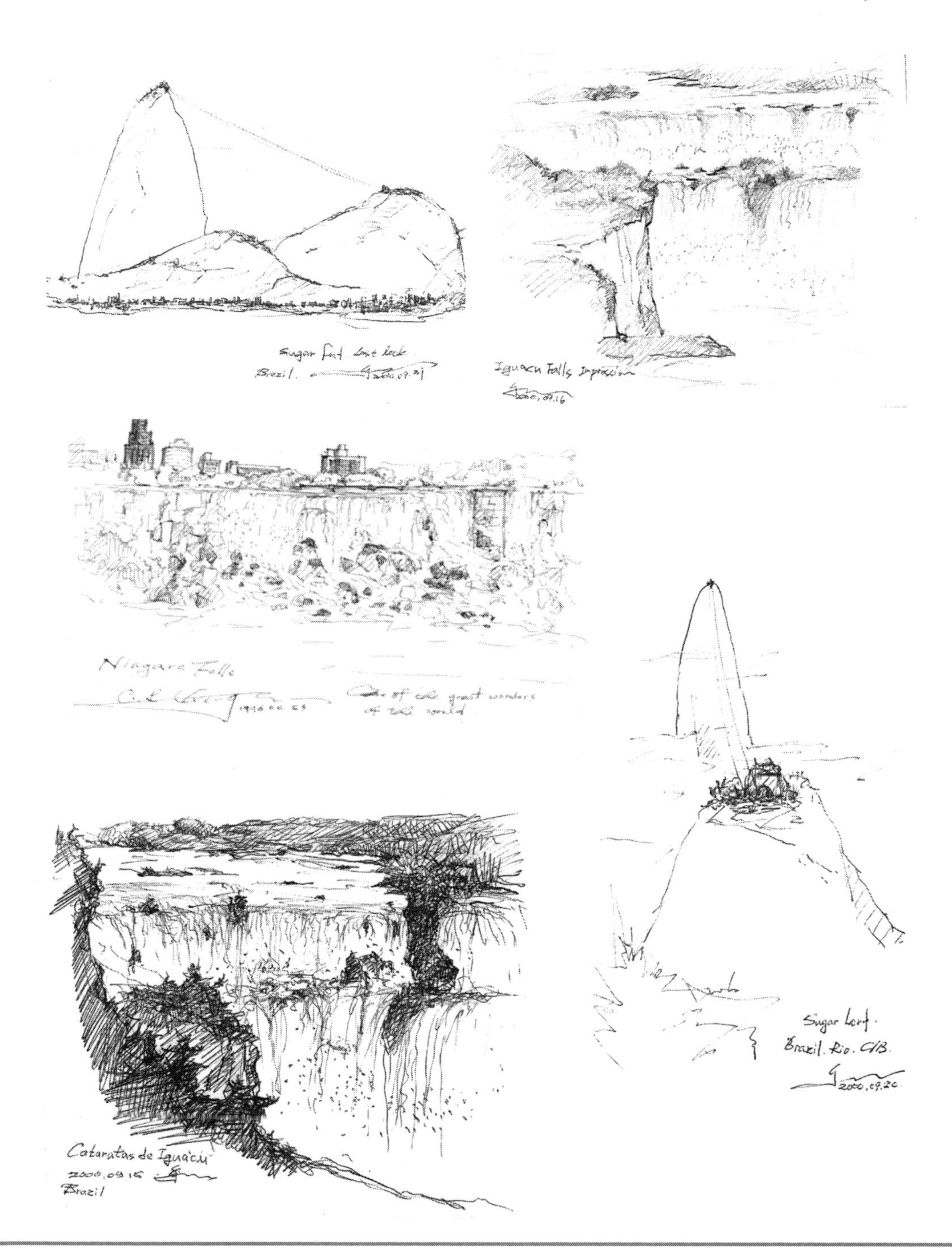
Brazil.
Iguacu Falls Impression
Niagara Falls
Sugar Loaf.
Brazil. Rio.
Cataratas de Iguaçu
Brazil

Sugar Loaf. Rio Janeiro.
Brazil.
Corcovado.
Sugar Loaf. Rio. Brazil
Sugar Loaf. Rio.
Corcovado. Rio. Janeiro. Brazil.
Corcovado. Rio. Janeiro.
of the world.
Brazil.

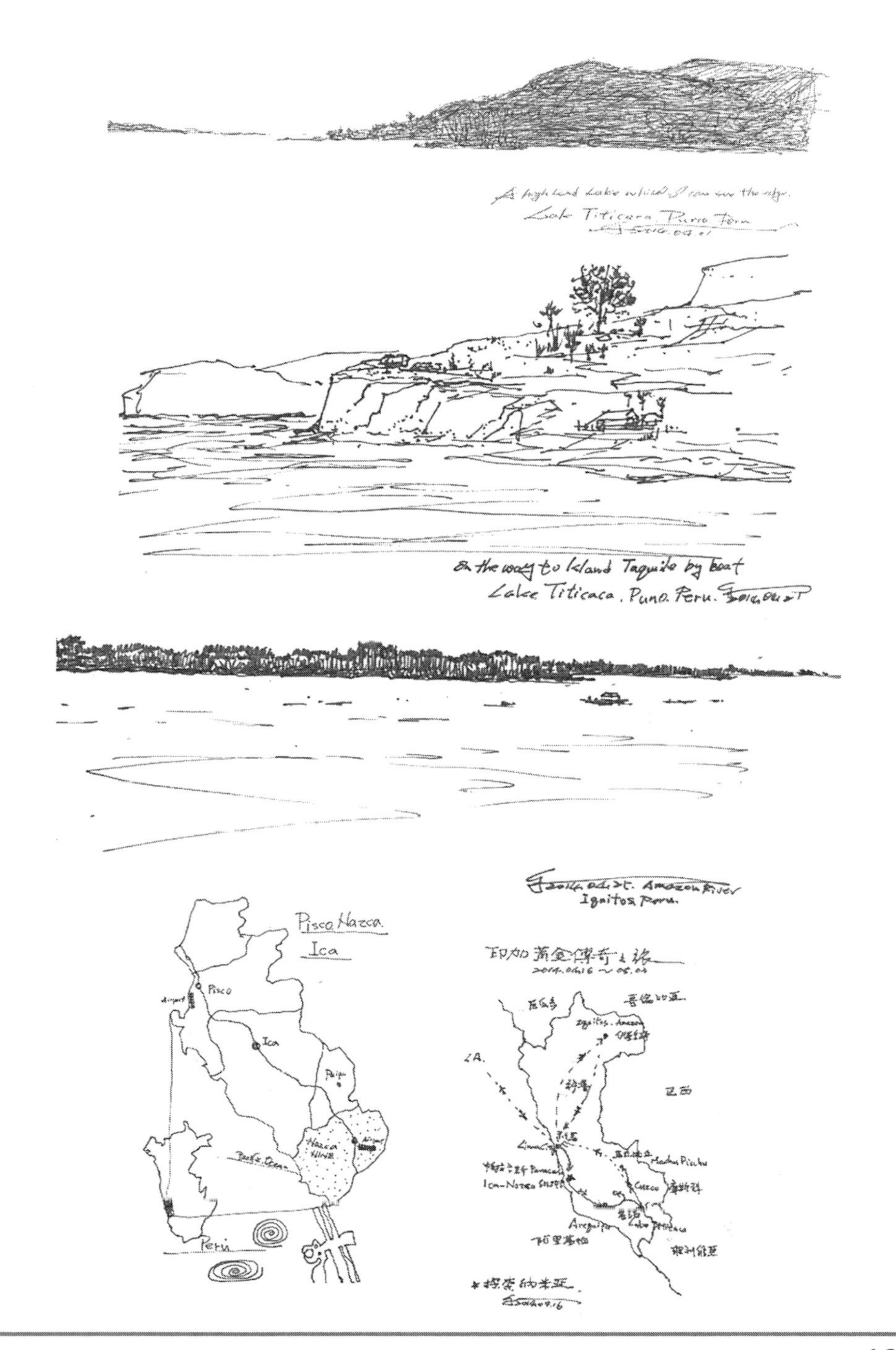
Lake Titicaca Puno Peru
On the way to Island Taquile by boat
Lake Titicaca. Puno. Peru.
Amazon River
Igaitos Peru.
Pisco Nazca
Ica
Pisco
Ica
Peru
印加黃金傳奇之旅
2014.04.16 ~ 05.04
L.A.
Cusco
Machu Picchu
Arequipa

Lima. Peru.
Beach city
Misti Volcano
Arequipa Peru
2014.04.20
CONDOR PERU

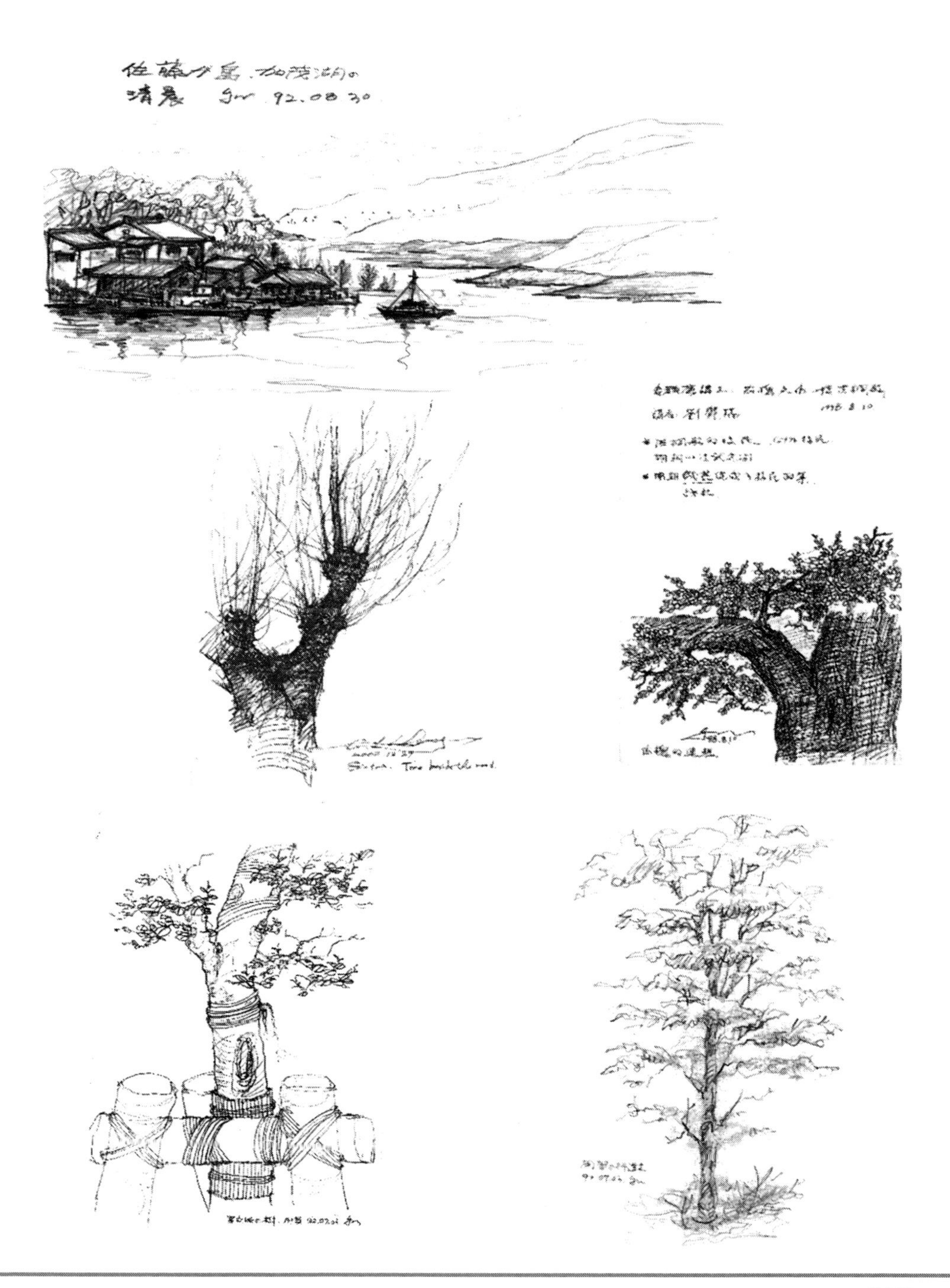

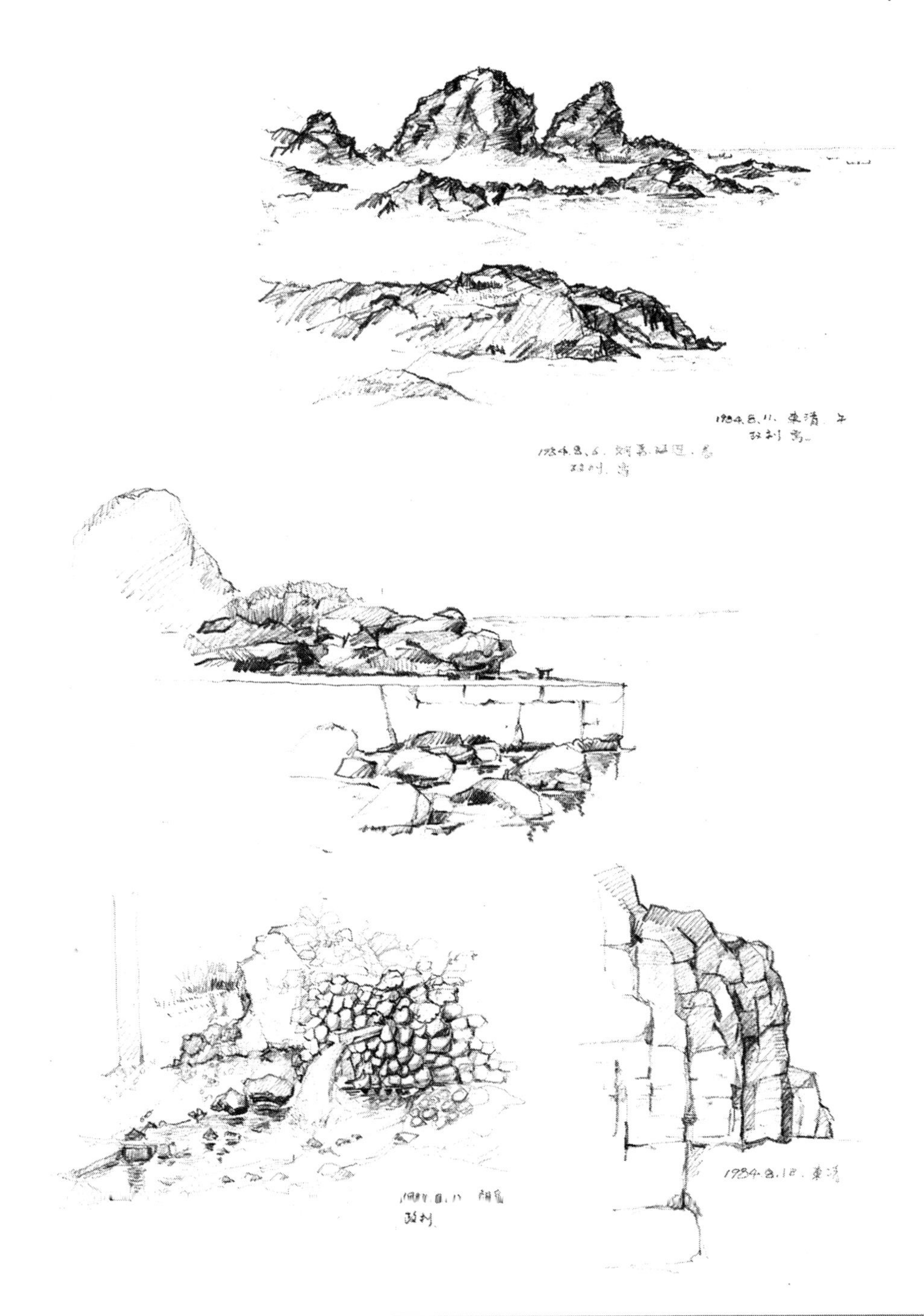
1984.8.11. 東清
1984.8.18. 東清

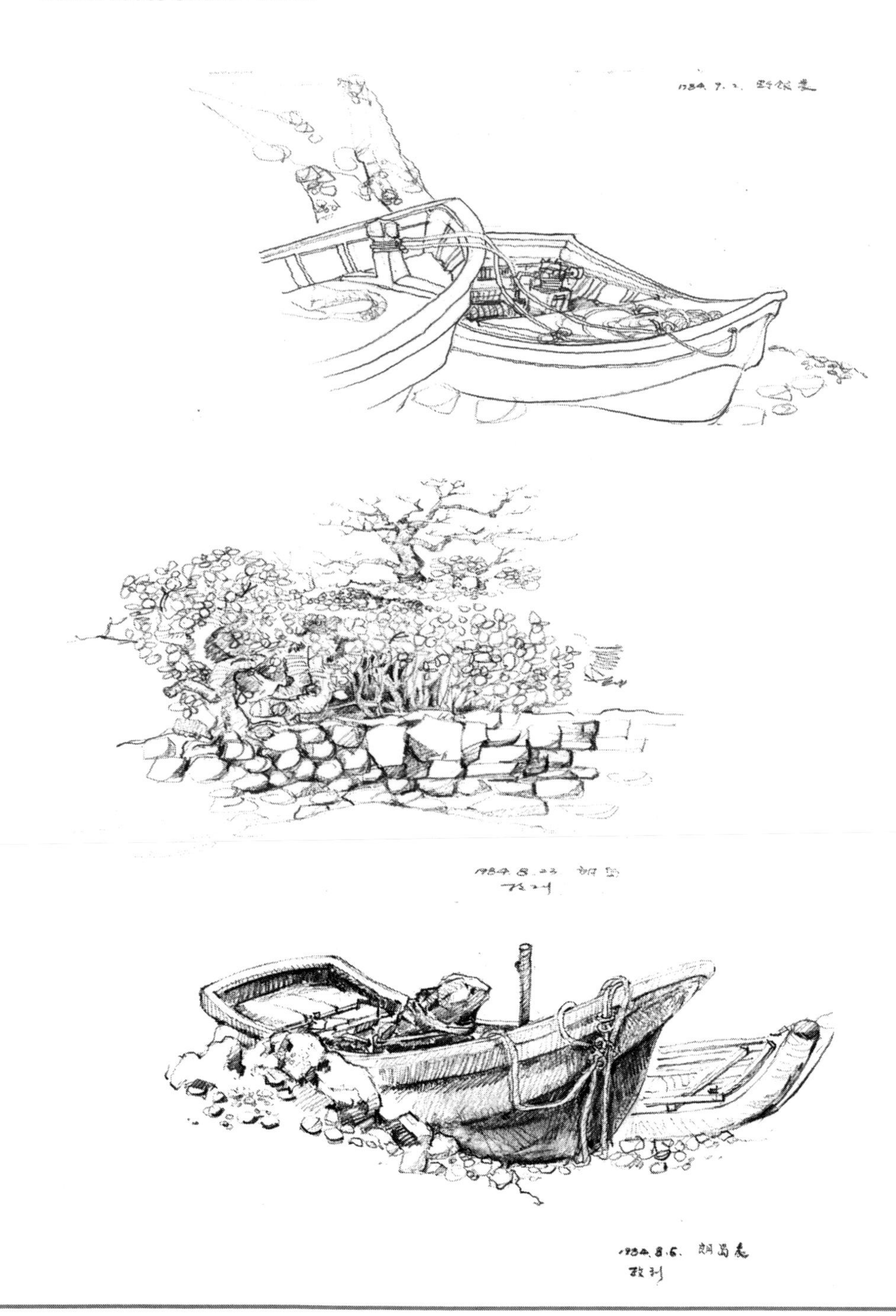

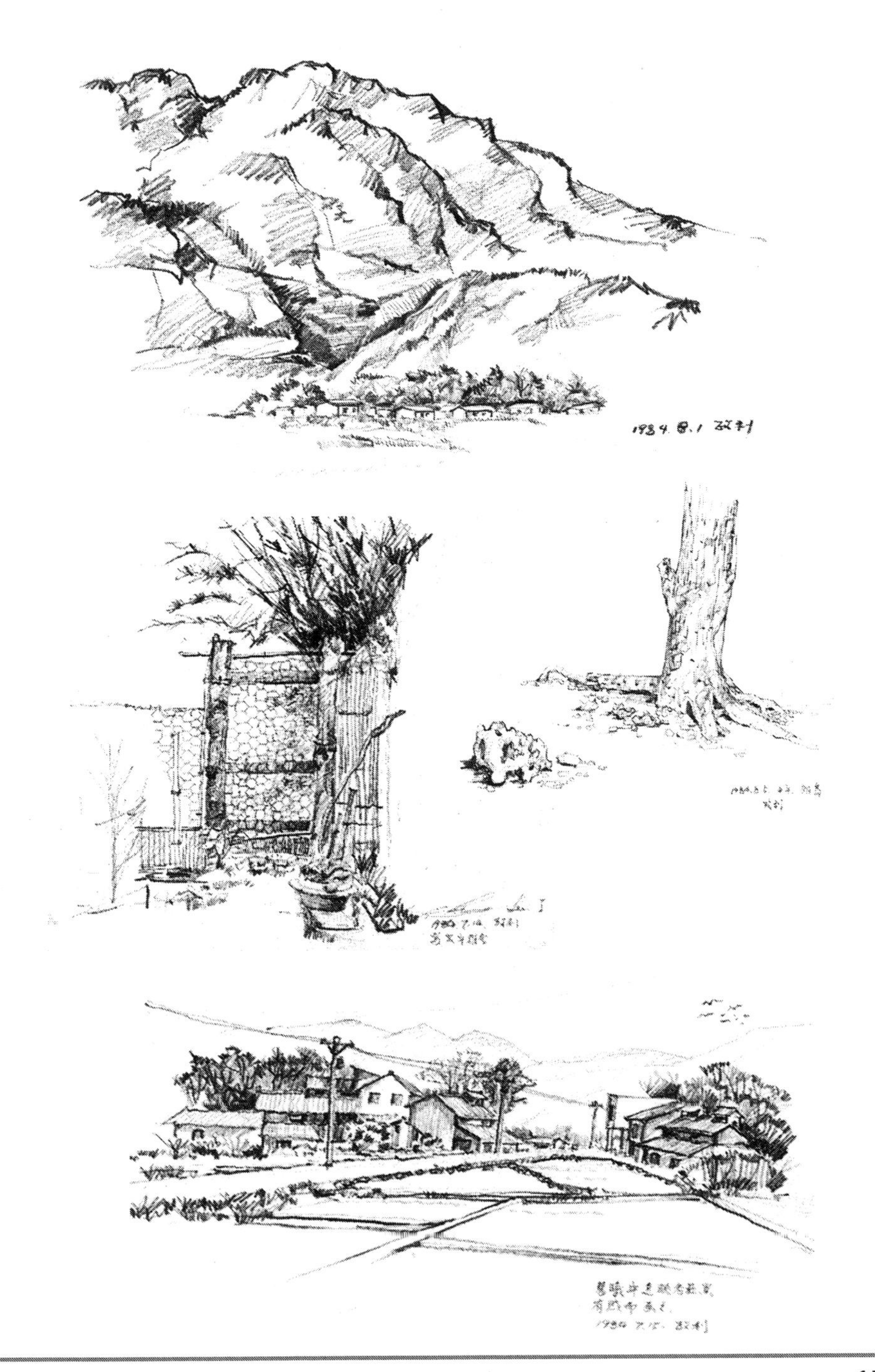

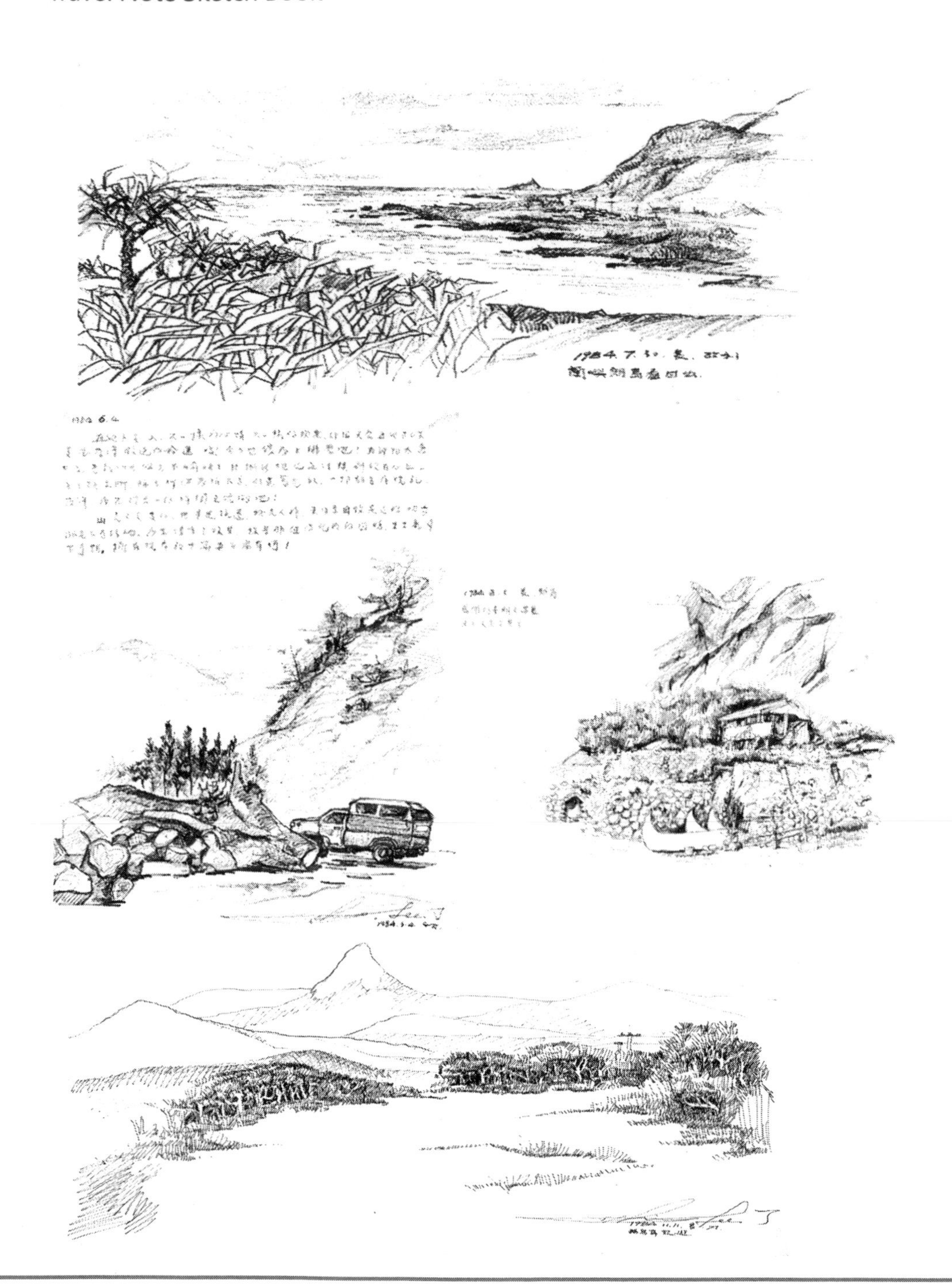

Flower drawing from
Mackintosh. Glasgow

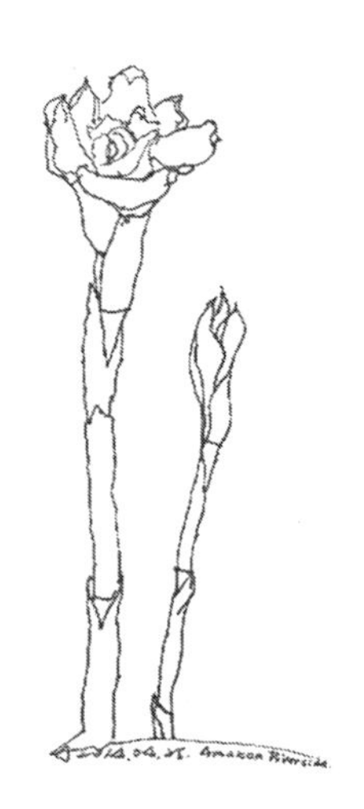
Amazon Riverside

山上会館
窗前等待春天
的樹、龍岡門
別館
2001.02.17

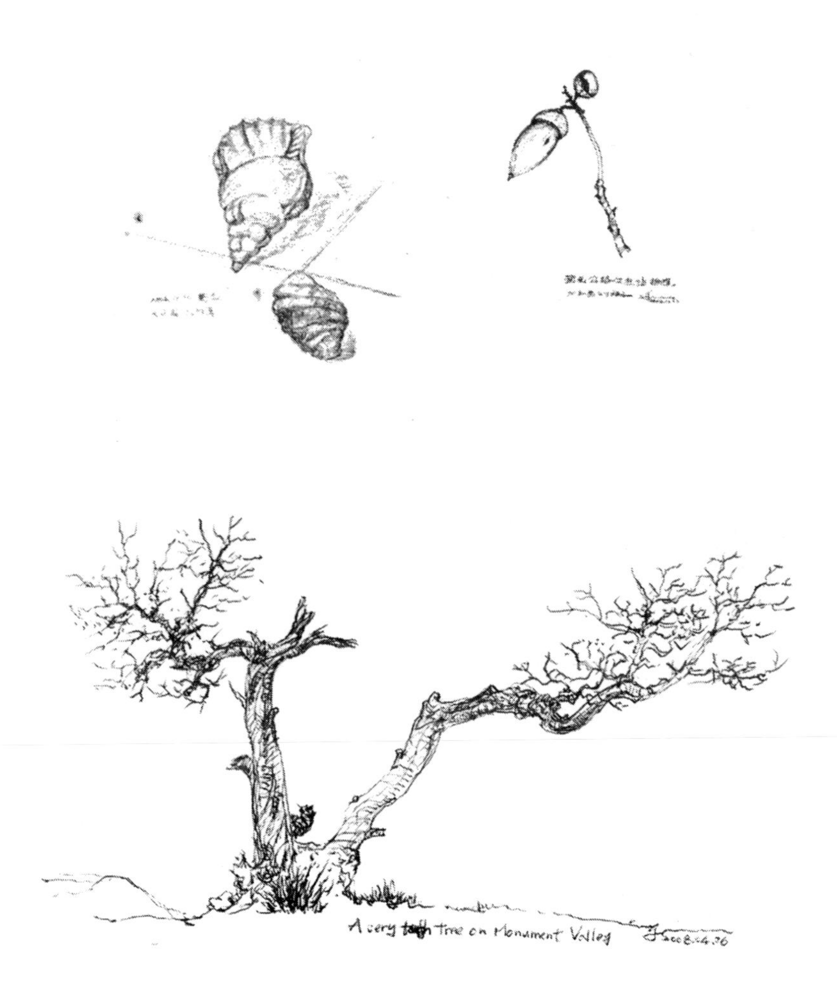
A very tough tree on Monument Valley
2008.4.26

想像

Imagination

有時候在旅行中，當周遭具體的形象事物不再能滿足畫筆的渴望時，讓自由線條隨興地在畫紙上遊走，不拘泥於細節形體，任其自由發展成形，這時候往往會有令人意想不到的驚奇與樂趣……

Sometimes as traveling, when the surrounding definite images can no longer satisfy the desire of the brush, let the free lines walk on the drawing paper freely, not constrained by the details, and let it develop and take shape freely. Then some unexpected surprise and funny images would appear.....

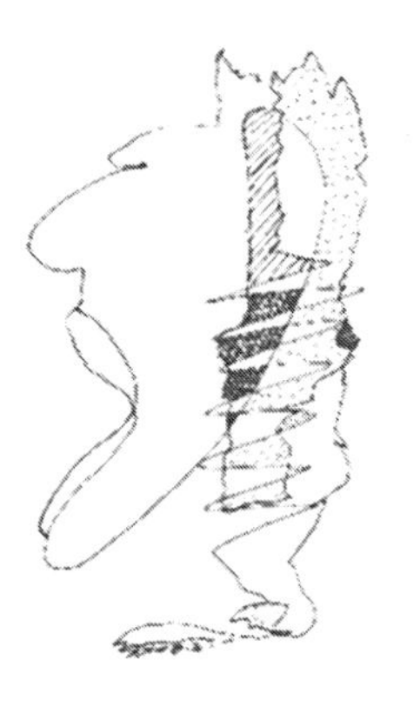

2020.11.27

2018.02.25
2019.02.16

2015.06.18
2015.06.16
2015.06.18

2015.06.21
2015.06.20

2015.06.21
2015.08.31

2015.09.29
2015.09.29
2015.09.29
2015.11.07
2015.11.07

2015.11.10
2018.06.17

2016.06.22
2016.06.22

2016.10.01
2016.10.29
2016.10.29
2016.10.29

2017.04.15
2017.04.15
2017.04.15
2018.02.21.
2018.02.21
2018.02.21

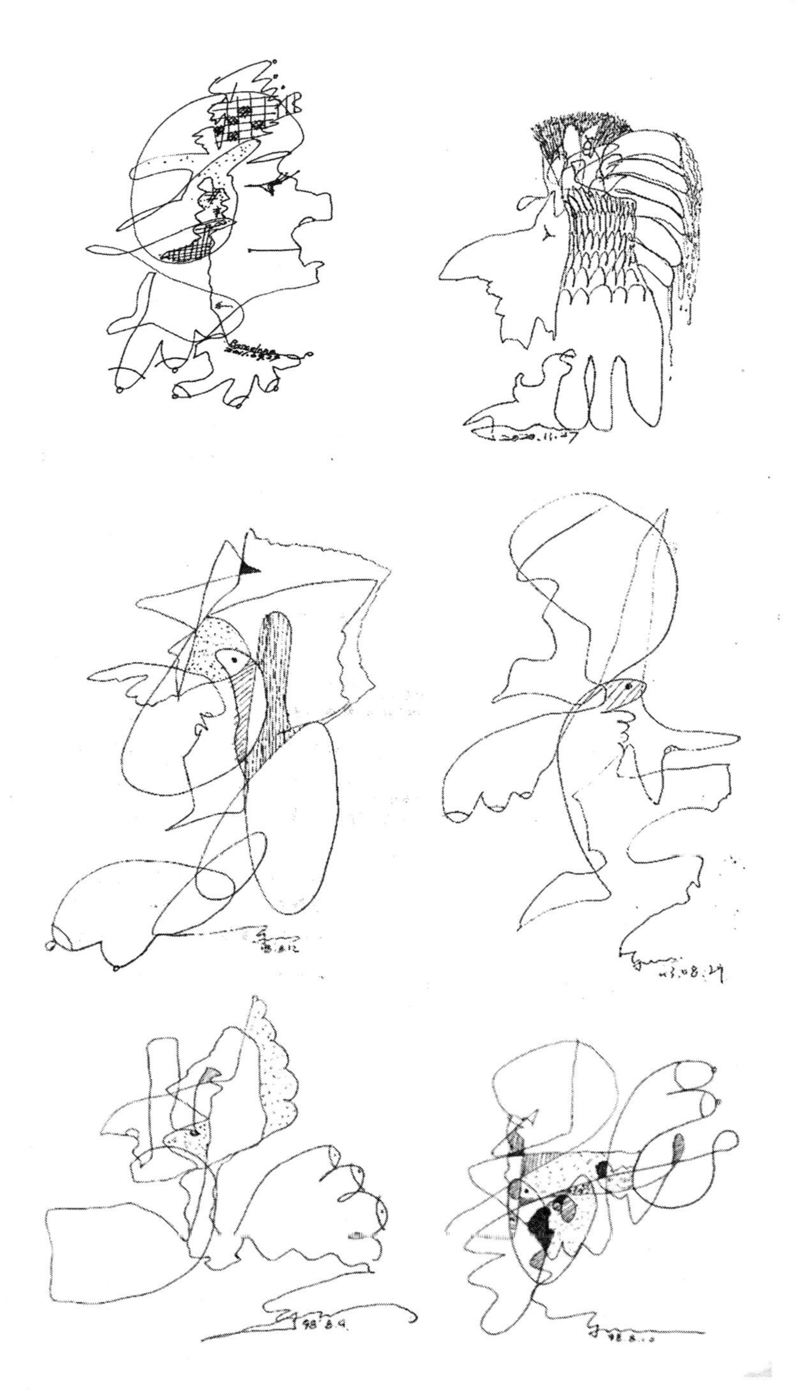

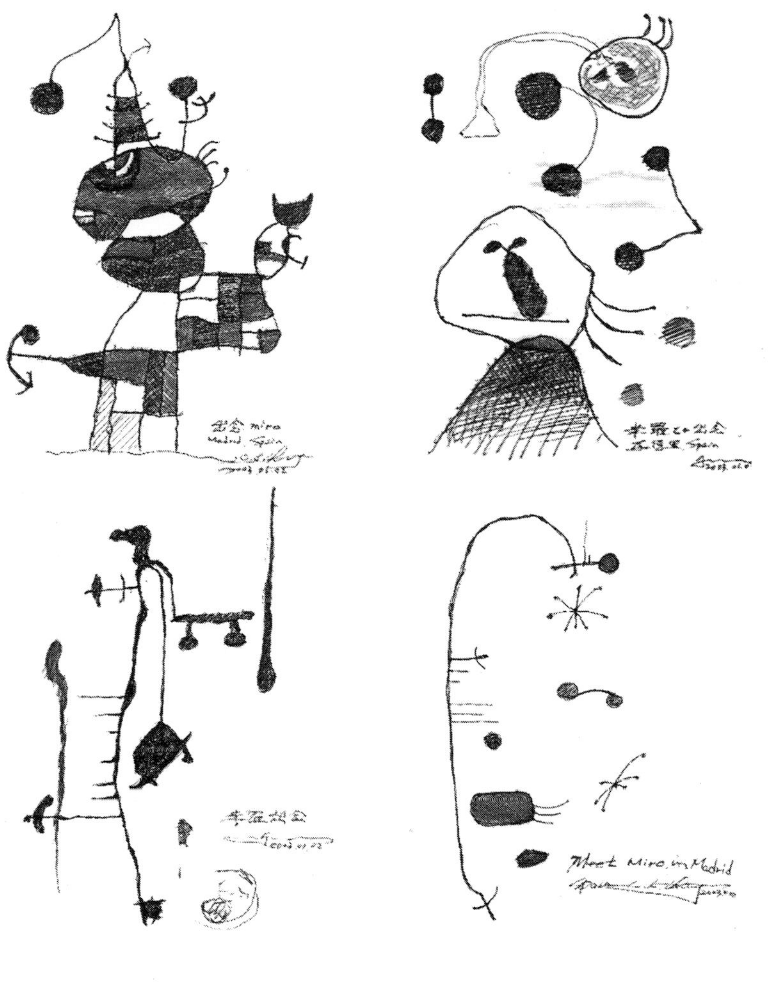

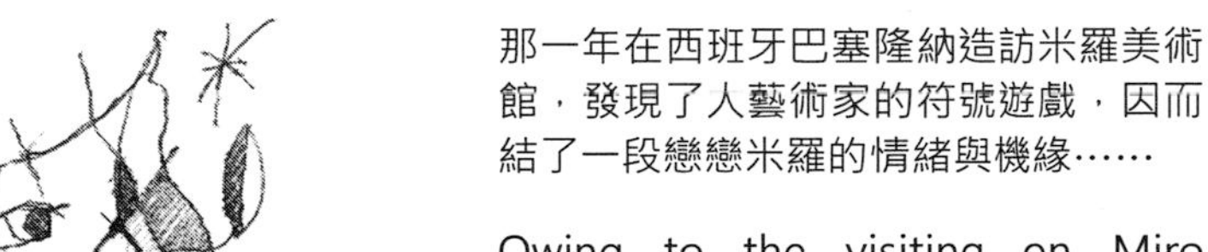

那一年在西班牙巴塞隆納造訪米羅美術館，發現了人藝術家的符號遊戲，因而結了一段戀戀米羅的情緒與機緣⋯⋯

Owing to the visiting on Miro Museum, I found the great artist’ s symbolic game. Consequently, a period of Miro emotion was created from this journey......

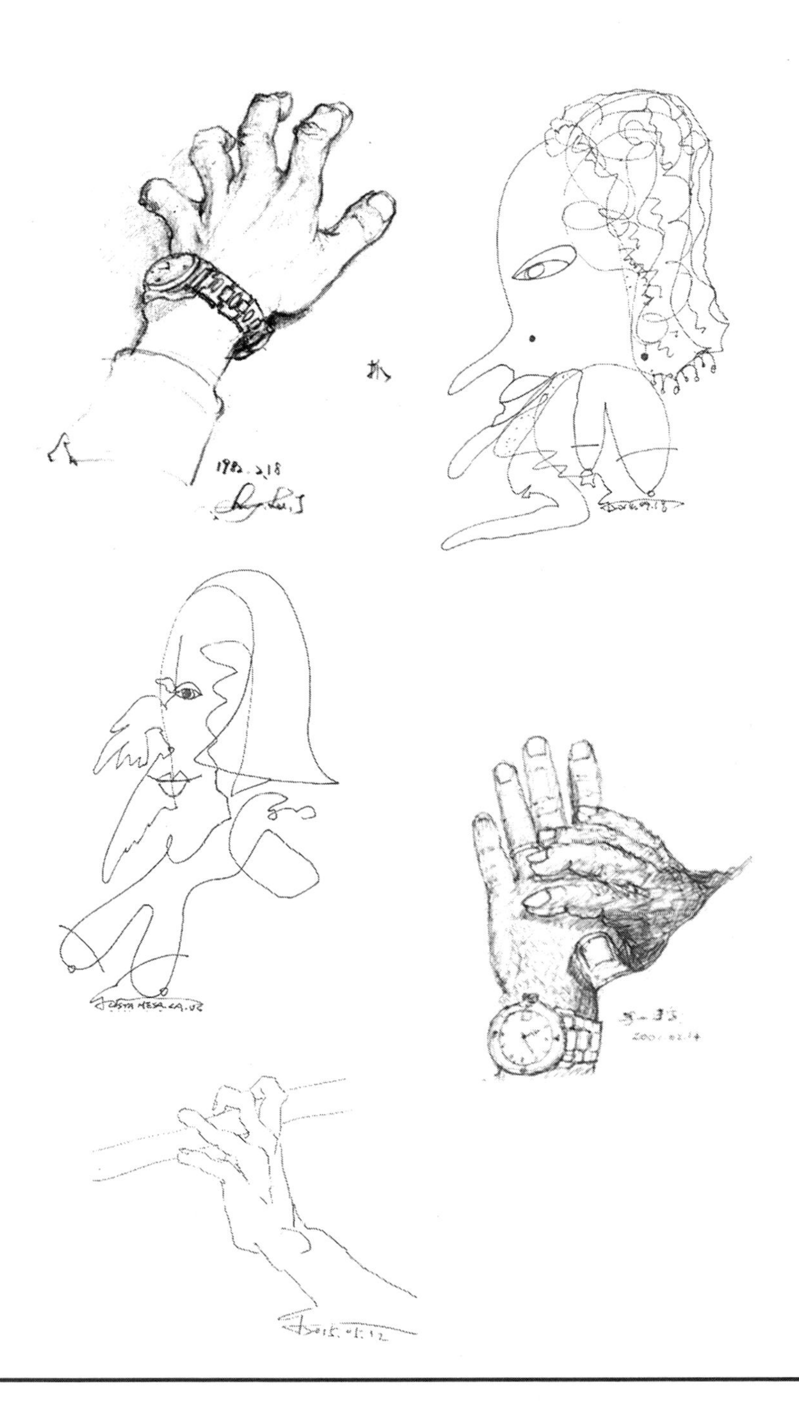

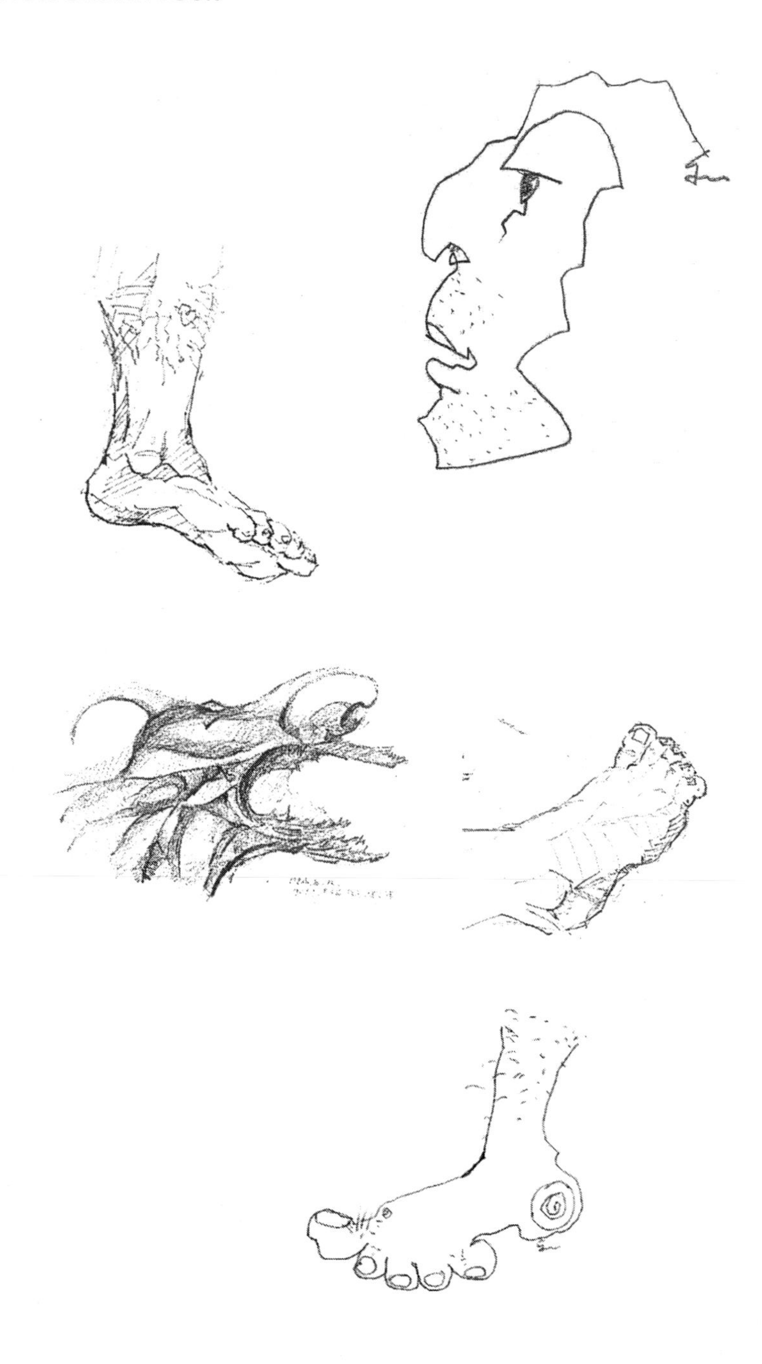

國家圖書館出版品預行編目資料

建築旅行：旅行速寫簿／鄭政利　著.－初版.－
臺中市：天空數位圖書　2021.02
面：17X23 公分
ISBN：978-986-5575-24-3（平裝）

863.55　　　　　　　　　　　110001650

書　　名：建築旅行：旅行速寫簿
發 行 人：蔡秀美
出 版 者：天空數位圖書有限公司
著 作 人：鄭政利
版面編輯：採編組
美工設計：設計組
出版日期：2021 年 02 月（初版）
銀行名稱：合作金庫銀行南台中分行
銀行帳戶：天空數位圖書有限公司
銀行帳號：006-1070717811498
郵政帳戶：天空數位圖書有限公司
劃撥帳號：22670142
定　　價：新台幣 360 元整
電子書發明專利第　I　306564 號

Family Sky
紙本書編輯印刷：
電子書編輯製作：
天空數位圖書公司 E-mail：familysky@familysky.com.tw　http://www.familysky.com.tw/
地址：台中市忠明南路787號30樓　Tel:04-22623893　Fax:04-22623863